CHICAGO P.D., HOMICIDE

By Robert R. Railey

ISBN: 978-1-62249-232-9
Library of Congress Control Number: 2014921913

Published by
The Educational Publisher
Biblio Publishing
BiblioPublishing.com

TABLE OF CONTENTS

A Near Miss

Chapter One

In the beginning

Al Capone didn't necessarily believe that it was a disgrace to be poor; he did however, think that it was a great inconvenience. Capone had learned early on to appreciate the finer things in life and so when he began looking around for a way out of his poverty he found that crime does sometimes pay.

Capone began his life in crime as a bouncer in a New York City nightclub where one evening, while working a wedding party for a fellow mobster, his face was permanently scarred by a razor while he was attempting to break up a barroom brawl between a man and a woman; and then shortly thereafter, he was investigated by the police on a charge of homicide. From then on, Capone was constantly being hauled in by the New York City Police Department on numerous and nefarious charges which included racketeering, suspicion of murder, and carrying a concealed weapon; the latter being a charge for which he would ultimately spend some time in jail.

But when New York City got too hot for him Capone very wisely decided to move to Chicago, Illinois where he wasn't quite as well known by the police; and in due time, he went to work for a Chicago mobster by the name of

Johnny Torrio who was a known associate of Capone's former Mafia boss back in New York City.

However, after having spent only a relatively short period of time in the city of Chicago, Capone killed Torrio; this then ultimately gave him complete control of all the criminal activities on the Southside of Chicago.

Therefore, the only other person still left standing in Capone's way of becoming the undisputed crime boss of the entire city of Chicago was a bootlegger on the North Side of town by the name of Bugs Moran. Eventually, however, future events would put Capone at odds with that notorious bootlegger.

Although just prior to the advent of prohibition, the various law enforcement agencies in the Chicago area had regarded the business of bootlegging as only a minor nuisance; but all that would change when in the year of nineteen hundred and nineteen the United States Congress passed into law a new bill known as the Volstead Act.

Accordingly then, and seemingly almost as if by overnight, it'd suddenly become a Federal crime to sell alcoholic beverages to the general public. Unbeknownst to the members of the United States Congress, however, they'd inadvertently left the door open for the bootlegging gangsters of America to manufacture and sell their illegal wares of liquor; and so from then on it would be up to a special group of Federal Agents such as Elliot Ness and others to put the bootleggers out of business.

Though at that point in time the Federal Agents weren't the only ones who were wreaking havoc upon the bootleggers of America since the mobsters were already doing a pretty job of destroying one another themselves. And so within only a few years following the inception of the new law over four hundred of the bootlegging mobsters had already been murdered in the city of

Chicago alone; and also not so surprisingly, the Chicago land newspaper journalist were predicting that the total number of gangland slayings might even exceed the five hundred mark before the National Prohibition Act would eventually be repealed by the newly elected American President Franklin Delano Roosevelt and his fellow Democrats who in the year of nineteen hundred and thirty-three had taken over control of the United States Congress.

22
CHICAGO POLICE
DETECTIVE SERGT.
URBS IN HORTO

Chapter Two

Plans That Go Awry

During the early years of prohibition when Al Capone and all the rest of the Chicago land bootleggers were still trying to make their first millions, a lawyer and a former Chicagoan by the name of George Remus, had already made a small fortune in the city of Cincinnati, Ohio by representing bootleggers and murderers.

Eventually, however, Remus couldn't help but notice that many of his bootlegging clients had become very wealthy in a relatively short period of time. And therefore, Remus proceeded to buy up all of the legal distilleries in the state of Ohio where, at the time, a whopping eighty percent of all the liquor in America was being produced.

Then during those early years of prohibition Remus had managed to gain control of all the illegal liquor that was being sold in the Cincinnati area. And during that period of time he'd become successful beyond his wildest dreams. In fact, it's been estimated that George Remus had earned at least forty million dollars during a three year span.

It was also during those early days of prohibition when Remus, and his right-hand man George Conners, discussed the possibility of expanding their bootlegging empire beyond the Cincinnati area and very possibly even reaching out as far as Chicago, Illinois.

"Since we already control around eighty percent of all the alcoholic spirits being produced in the United States, I don't see why the bootleggers in the city of Chicago shouldn't buy their liquor from us instead of those mobs up in Canada," said George Remus.

"In some respects, I tend to agree with you; however, we must remember that the Italian gangs have a long and sordid history of either making a person sell their businesses to them at a much lower dollar value, or else they just simply kill off the owners and then take over the businesses for themselves," said Conner.

"Perhaps you're right, we might be better off just staying right where we are," said Remus.

Nevertheless, back in the year of nineteen hundred and twenty-nine it was still business as usual for the bootlegging gangsters of Chicago, who by then, were producing as much of the illegal liquor as the local drinking public could ever possibly consume; and it was also during that same period of time that a notorious mobster by the name of Charles Vincente was gainfully employed as a Capo, or captain, in Al Capone's mob.

But then on the eve of St. Valentine's Day of that very same year, the rules of gang warfare were about to change when Al Capone ordered his Lieutenants and Captains to attend an early morning meeting which was scheduled to be held at Capone's motel which was located in the Chicago suburb of Cicero, Illinois.

Accordingly then, it was at that early morning meeting that a gangster by the name of Charles Vincente was given orders to take care of some troublesome people for Capone; and it was also at that very same meeting when Capone told his fellow mobsters that it was imperative for him to be in his mansion in Florida on the day that his North Side bootlegging competitors were to be eliminated.

Vincente had just received his third assignment of the month and the first two examples of his deadly work were already dead and buried in Park Lawn Cemetery. And as previously planned, Al Capone was indeed resting comfortably at his Southern estate on that fateful day in February; but, he wasn't there solely for the sunshine. Capone was in Florida on that particular day because the St. Valentine's Day Massacre was scheduled to take place on the North Side of Chicago and he needed desperately to have a solid alibi when the murders were being committed.

22
CHICAGO POLICE
DETECTIVE SERGT.
URBS IN HORTO

Chapter Three

Missed Opportunities

As fate would have it, Charles Vincente didn't eventually stagger up the two flights of stairs to his small apartment in Cicero, Illinois until the wee early morning hours of St. Valentine's Day; it'd been a long hard day and night.

Vincente was in a foul mood that morning and he was still more than a little intoxicated from the night before which might have caused him to become a little too easily aggravated with his wife for taking so much time in the preparation of his breakfast.

Vincente was a brutish sort of a man with men and women alike: he'd once read an old English Proverb which stated, "A woman a dog a walnut tree, the more you beat them the better they be," and that suited him just fine. Vincente also fervently believed that women were good for just two things; one of those was cooking, and then of course, there was the other.

And just like any good practicing drunk might do, Vincente hurriedly finished drinking a cup of Prohibition Whiskey before once again reaching for the bottle; but then as he did so, his wife commented that by the looks of him that he didn't appear to need any more whiskey on that particular morning.

The whiskey, along with his own natural animalistic instincts must have compelled Charles to grab his wife by her nightgown and in a sudden violent rage he proceeded to slam her head into the plastered kitchen wall with such force as to render her unconscious. Then not so unexpectedly, it wasn't long before several representatives of the local village police department were banging loudly on the apartment door with their nightsticks.

Charles Vincente was then summarily hauled off to jail: and it wasn't until much later that same morning before he was allowed to appear in front of a bond magistrate; by then, however, he was already seriously late for a very important early morning meeting.

According to Vincente's boss, just the act of being tardy wasn't only a Cardinal Sin but it was an infraction that could prove to be fatal to a man; and Vincente's failure to show up for that early morning meeting was especially crucial to the prospects of his future health since it was St. Valentine's Day and there was work to be done.

Chapter Four

To flee or not to flee

Eventually, though, Vincente was allowed to post bond for the assault and battery charge against his wife; and then once free from his jail cell he very quickly made his way out of the Cook County Courthouse where he proceeded to hurriedly walk the two blocks to a drugstore where he could make his rounds of telephone calls.

But then once in the drugstore he really began to sweat when no one answered the telephone at either his, or his underboss's apartment. Therefore, Charles had to only assume that his fellow mobsters had gone on ahead without him.

By then, however, Charles was so completely distraught and beside himself for having missed out on that very important early morning rendezvous with his underlings that he staggered over to the soda fountain where he ordered a Bromo-seltzer with water. But as he was drinking his hangover helper he just happened to overhear a news report on the radio which stated that an incident which included multiple homicides had just taken place over on the North Side of town.

"Son of a bitch," Vincente shouted, and the glass in his hand suddenly shattered when he slammed it down too forcefully onto the counter top. At that moment, Charles knew full well that he was in big trouble with the boss; and he also realized that he had but few choices to make. First, he could try to hide out in the city: but then of course he knew that a decision of that nature could end up being very dangerous. But after giving the situation a few moments of due consideration he then very wisely came to the proper conclusion that the smartest thing for him to do would be to leave town.

So immediately after exiting the drugstore Charles continued to walk due-south until he eventually arrived at a pawnshop where he knew that he would be able to purchase a handgun.

Vincente had assumed, and rightfully so, that the man he worked for would eventually find him if he decided to stay in the city of Chicago; and therefore, he knew there was only one logical decision left open for him to make so he hailed a taxicab. Then after first showing the cab driver the 45 caliber automatic pistol that he'd tucked away in his belt, Vincente placed up a hundred dollar bill in the cabby's hand with orders to drive him to Gary, Indiana.

Chapter Five

The Carnage

Because of the dozens of haphazardly parked police cars and ambulances on the streets and sidewalks surrounding the site of the massacre, Detective Sergeant James Morris of the Chicago Police Department's Homicide Division was forced to park almost a block away from the scene of the crime. Though once on the scene, James very quickly then learned that the slaughter had actually taken place on the interior of a garage which had formerly been owned by a cartage company. In recent years, however, the building had been primarily used as a warehouse where the notorious bootlegger Bugs Moran kept much of his illegal liquor.

From past experiences with similar such situations, James knew that the fastest way to learn the facts about a new case was to first locate the uniformed police Sergeant in charge of the crime scene; and the Sergeant he found was standing guard at the front door of the old cartage company.

"What's you got Sarge?" James asked.

"Detective it's the worst massacre I've seen since World War One," the Sergeant said.

"Are there any witnesses?" James asked.

"The people in the upstairs apartment across the street were the first ones to call it in: but detective you ain't seen nothing yet, and you're sure as hell not going to believe what the witnesses told us. They said that when the gunfire ended they saw several uniformed Chicago Policemen exit the front of the warehouse and then drive away in a police car," the Sergeant said.

All told, it would take three ambulances to haul away the mutilated bodies of the slaughtered bootleggers. Nonetheless, James was somewhat amazed that the body of Bugs Moran wasn't among the carnage: it looked like a near miss.

Then too, because of his past experiences with similar such circumstances, James was well aware of the importance of staying on good terms with the brass: and so he immediately then placed calls to his Lieutenant and Captain back at the stationhouse; but he also called a friend of his who worked in the Chief of Detectives office just to fill him in on the facts concerning Chicago's latest gangland slaughter.

And being that James was the highest ranking officer at the scene of the crime he knew that his primary job was to preserve the evidence; and so he immediately ordered that all of the uniformed police officers and the newspapermen should stay out of the garage until the coroner's office had completed their investigation. Then once that task had been completed, James and his partner, detective Donald Stevens, began canvassing the people who lived in the nearby surrounding neighborhood.

At such an early stage in their investigation, the two detectives knew that their main responsibility was to take statements from as many of the witnesses as possible in the hopes that someone had seen something other than those alleged police officers who'd purportedly been seen leaving the scene of the crime.

Then not so coincidentally, it was also around that same time of the morning when Al Capone received the phone call that he'd been waiting for; and then shortly thereafter he was aboard a private airplane headed for the city of Chicago.

Chapter Six

The escape

Also later on that same day, but many miles to the east of Chicago, Charles Vincente exited the taxicab near the front door of the Lowe's' Hotel in downtown Gary, Indiana. And after first tipping the cab driver an extra twenty dollars just to keep his mouth shut, he checked into the hotel. But instead of going directly to his room he walked out of the rear of the hotel and headed for the nearest department store where he planned on purchasing several changes of wardrobe, which among other items, would include a pair of work boots, a sailor's watch cap, and a pea coat.

Then once he'd completed his shopping, Vincente made his way back to the hotel room where he hurriedly changed his clothing before taking a taxicab to the train station in downtown Gary where he was planning on boarding a train that was headed for St. Louis, Missouri. Then once off the train in St. Louis he was planning on riding a city bus to the Greyhound Bus Station where he would once again change his clothes before boarding a bus headed for Kansas City, Missouri.

No one in Kansas City would recognize his face, Charles thought, and he hoped that by changing his name he might be able to find work in the coalmines like his ancestors had done when they'd first migrated to the state of Pennsylvania before then ultimately moving on to Chicago.

22
CHICAGO POLICE
DETECTIVE SERGT.
URBS IN HORTO

Chapter Seven

The Paper Trail

Janice (Tsjvold) Vincente was a blonde-haired, blue-eyed stunning beauty from a long line of Scandinavian descendants: and just four scant years prior to her latest and hopefully last visit to the hospital, she'd lived on a farm on the outskirts of a small river town in the Eastern part of the state of Iowa. But then after earning a two-year associate degree in the field of accounting from a community college in her hometown, Janice had made the momentous decision to move to Chicago, Illinois where she'd been offered a job in the main offices of the Sears & Roebuck Company.

Regrettably though, and as circumstances and events can sometimes portend, it'd just barely been a little over four years prior to that early morning altercation with Charles that Janice, and a few of the other girls in her office at Sears, had decided to visit one of the many speakeasies in the city of Chicago just so they could learn how to dance the Charleston which was a new craze that was rapidly sweeping across the nation.

Unfortunately for Janice, however, it was also at that very same speakeasy where she would meet her future husband, Charles Vincente.

Nevertheless, just a few short years following her unwise decision to marry the man she'd met in the speakeasy, Janice had once again been badly beaten and bruised. At least this time, however, she was thankful that her injuries were no more serious than they were; and even though she was told that she would have to wear a cervical collar around her neck for a while she knew that she was lucky to be alive.

On the other hand, though, Janice had begun to wonder if she would be as lucky the next time that Charles came home drunk: and so immediately upon her release from the hospital she made what might have been one of the most important decisions of her young life; and that was simply to get as far away from Charles Vincente as she possibly could.

Of course once the decision had been made to flee, then one of the first thing she had to attend to that morning was to withdraw her money from a personal and secret bank account; and then once that exercise had been completed she rode the city bus system from Cicero, Illinois to the train station in downtown Chicago where she planned on boarding the first train leaving for St. Louis, Missouri; and then once in St. Louis, she knew that it would be a simple matter for her to catch a Greyhound bus which would ultimately deliver her back to her hometown in Iowa.

All throughout the long four years of her marriage to Charles, and then just shortly after the physical abuse had begun to worsen, Janice had desperately wanted to leave him. Unfortunately for her, however, he'd told her numerous times, and in no uncertain terms, that he would track her down and kill her if she ever did try to leave.

And even though Janice sincerely believed that Charles would most likely try to kill her if she ever did leave him, she was constantly looking for a way out of her dangerous situation; but then after having suffered physical abuse for the better part of four years she'd begun to keep records of some of his more notorious criminal activities just in case he decided to come after her if and when she ever got up the nerve to leave him for good.

Nevertheless, providence must have been shinning down on Janice that morning because no sooner had she'd realized that Charles was tucked safely away in a jail cell did she fully understand that her only real chance for freedom had finally come.

Also earlier that same morning, but only after the police had hauled Charles off to jail, Janice had the foresight to gather up a few of her personal belongings before she would allow the medical personnel to take her off to the hospital; and in addition to packing a few pieces of clothing and some personal effects, she'd also remembered to gather up some of Charles's criminal business records that he'd unwittingly left lying on top of the kitchen table when the police had so abruptly hauled him off to jail.

Then all throughout that long train ride from Chicago to St. Louis Janice was still desperately clutching the large manila envelope to her chest which contained a multitude of the self-incriminating notes and scraps of paper that Vincente had written during those hundreds of hours of telephone conversations that he'd had with his criminal associates during the past four years that Janice had lived with him.

Then too, all throughout those same four years of her volatile marriage to Charles, but with her thoughts ultimately on her own personal safety, Janice had secretly written down as many of the private telephone conversations as she possibly could have anytime that she had the opportunity to listen in on him while he was talking on the phone to his fellow mobsters.

And even though Janice had saved many of those potentially incriminating pieces of secretly hand-written telephone conversations, the one item in particular that she'd found the most intriguing was the doodling on a scrap of paper on which Charles had scribbled a short list of names but had unintentionally left lying on the top of the kitchen table when the police took him off to jail.

What'd made that one singular piece of potential evidence seem so interesting to Janice was simply the fact that two of the men whose names were on the list had just recently been murdered; and consequently, their names had been scratched off the list; this then left the sole name of Bugs Moran.

In Janice's way of thinking, if Charles ever did try to follow her back to her childhood home in Iowa then perhaps the criminal records that she had in her possession might just possibly be enough of an insurance policy to keep him from killing her; or at least, that's what she was hoping for.

Chapter Eight

Safe and Sound

Needless to say, Janice was genuinely happy to be back home in Iowa with her friends and family who she knew were the most caring and honest people on the face of the earth. Janice was also a tad bit ashamed of herself for thinking that true happiness could only be found in the bright lights of the big city when in reality she knew without a doubt that the people back home were the best people she'd ever known. Janice's father had always credited those worthwhile family traits to the blood ties they'd once had with the Vikings of old.

For according to the Tsjvold family history, before Janice's family had migrated to America, her ancestors had originally come from a country in Northern Europe where the Tsjvold family had always made their living as farmers; but then during that same period of time, there'd been a scarcity of good farmland in the whole of Scandinavia and so the Tsjvold family had made the decision to move to America where not only there was a great abundance of available and fertile farmland, but at that time the land in America was affordable to people of even modest means.

Nonetheless, it's also fair to say that Janice wasn't looking forward to hearing her parents say, "I told you so." Albeit, she vowed that she would be willing to do almost anything in order to stay away from the abusive man that she'd been married to for the past four years;

even if it meant that she might have to live with her parents for a while. Janice was also thinking that she might even marry that nice looking German neighbor of hers back home in Iowa who'd just recently become a widower.

Chapter Nine

Into the hunt

In the not too far distant past, and back when Detective Sergeant James Morris was still learning the ropes on how to become a proper homicide detective, he'd been singled out and highly decorated for "displaying an exemplary act of personal bravery which went above and beyond the call duty." The situation for which he'd been promoted had come about when one of Capone's hoodlums pulled a gun on him while he was trying to affect an arrest: and in the melee` that ensued James was forced to shoot to kill; and the end result of that devastating and frightening situation was that James was ultimately awarded the highly coveted Detective Sergeant's Gold Shield.

Also in addition to that one singular and traumatic life changing episode which had taken place when James still held the rank of Detective Corporal, he'd been instrumental in sending several of Capone's mobsters off to prison. So from that date forward both James and his partner, detective Donald Stevens, had made it a personal quest of theirs to take as many of Capone's gangsters off the streets of Chicago as they possibly could.

Therefore, since the St. Valentine's Day Massacre case had been so unceremoniously dumped in his lap, and also being that he knew most of the mobsters in the city Chicago by name and many of them by sight, James had mistakenly believed that it was going to be a simple matter for them to find the trigger men who were responsible for the city's latest massacre.

James knew that Charles Vincente was the man that normally handled most of Capone's gunmen, but he was also well aware of the fact that Vincente often worked closely with a gangster by the name of Frank Nitti who was another one of Capone's infamous killers.

Then just as James had assumed that it would be, that one spectacular and murderous fourteenth day of February in the year of nineteen hundred and twenty-nine had turned into a very long day and night; however, the day appeared as if it might even end up being longer when James stopped by at the nearest police callbox to check in with his Lieutenant back at the stationhouse and was told, "to bring in Capone for questioning: but if Capone couldn't be found then Charles Vincente would have to do."

So upon receiving the latest order from their boss, lieutenant Fernando Devillez, James and his partner immediately drove over to the village of Cicero where they rendezvoused with several uniformed deputies from the Cook County Sheriff's Department who proceeded to escort them to the walk-up flat where Vincente was purportedly living at the time; but then when nobody answered the knock at the apartment door, the two detectives were forced to locate the building superintendent who informed them of the early morning altercation which had not only resulted in Vincente being arrested, but also of the fact that his wife Janice had been taken off to one of the local hospitals.

Accordingly, then, James had only to make a quick phone call to the desk Sergeant at the district police station in order to confirm that Vincente had indeed been arrested earlier that same day; but then the very same desk

Sergeant told James that Charles had subsequently been released on bond. Moreover, when James phoned the hospital to check up on Janice Vincente's condition he was told that she'd been treated but that she too had already been released.

Consequently, the first full day into the investigation of the St. Valentine's Day Massacre was about to become even more stymied when only a few of the usual suspects could be located; but James knew full well that it was imperative for the police to pick up as many of Capone's known soldiers as quickly as possible since the gang wars would almost certainly intensify now that Capone had failed in his attempt to have Bugs Moran murdered.

22
CHICAGO POLICE
DETECTIVE SERGT.
URBS IN HORTO

Chapter Ten

The Quest

Then expressly because of the latest gang war between the two rival bootlegging gangs of Chicago, it was understandable that Detective Sergeant James Morris, and his partner detective Donald Stevens, were having trouble locating any of Capone's capos. Eventually, though, the two detectives were successful in finding at least a few of his underlings; and during one of those interrogations they learned that the man who was most responsible for the latest mayhem in the city Chicago had just recently landed at a private airport somewhere out in the Cook County countryside.

Then upon receiving that latest bit of useful information concerning the whereabouts of Al Capone, the two detectives decided to make another trip back to Vincente's apartment just in case the gangster had returned home, but he hadn't. Yet while at the apartment, James was able to pocket a few of Vincent's personal papers that were lying on top of the kitchen table.

Also fortunately for the two detectives, one of the letters that James was able to appropriate was addressed to Charles's wife, Janice Vincente. More importantly, though, that particular letter listed the return name and address of a family by the name of Tsjvold who apparently lived in a small town in the state of Iowa.

Then upon their arrival at the stationhouse the two detectives were fortunate enough to be able find a listing for the Tsjvold family in an Iowa telephone book; and when James contacted the family by telephone he learned that the names of the people on the envelope were indeed the parents of the missing woman they knew as Janice (Tsjvold) Vincente.

Unfortunately for James however, he then owned the unpleasant duty of having to inform the parents of the fact that their daughter was presumed to be missing and unaccounted for. So naturally, when the parents heard the disheartening news about their daughter they told James that even though they hadn't spoken with her for several days they'd been planning on making the trip to Chicago just so that they could rescue their daughter from an apparently hopeless situation.

But then after a few more minutes of nothing more than polite conversation, James told the parents that he would stay in touch with them. Nonetheless, he'd also made it a point to tell the parents of the missing woman that it was of the utmost importance that they should call him back just as soon as they heard from their daughter. James also asked the parents to please call him back if and when they ever received any information concerning the whereabouts of their son-in-law, Charles Vincente.

Chapter Eleven

The Wars

Then immediately upon his return from Florida, the first thing on Capone's agenda was to summon his Lieutenants and Captains together for a council of war; however, the one person he wished most to speak with was still missing. Yet earlier that same day after Vincente had failed to show up for the planned execution of the mob's rival bootleggers, two of Capone's soldiers had gone to his apartment to look for him. Consequently, it was when the mobsters were at the apartment that they'd first learned of Vincente's arrest; but then after they'd made some phone calls to a few of their acquaintances at the district police station, the hoodlums learned that even though Charles had subsequently been released on bond he'd vanished and he was still missing.

Although later on that same evening when the mobsters made a return visit to Vincente's apartment they were told by the superintendent that not only had the police been there looking for Charles, but that one of the detectives had actually removed some of his personal papers.

So in view of the importance of that latest piece of information regarding Vincente's mysterious vanishing act, Capone had to only assume that the police were in possession of some very incriminating evidence against him and Vincente.

A NEAR MISS

By then, Capone must have felt as if his situation was extremely tenuous and so he immediately then called for an emergency late night meeting with his Lieutenants. Then during that impromptu meeting, Capone appeared to be just as psychotic as he was at the time when he'd crushed in the skull of a fellow mobster with a baseball bat. To the other gangsters who were in attendance at the late night meeting it was apparent that Capone had hardened his views on the perception of his enemies: that is, if that was humanely possible to do so, for at the conclusion of his insane diatribe he proceeded to say to his fellow mobsters, "I want you to kill them all, especially Bugs Moran and Charles Vincente."

And even though the ill-fated gang wars had posed a severe threat to both the citizens of the city and the Chicago Police Department, it still took another two full weeks of gangland slaughter on both sides of town before a truce of sorts was finally agreed upon by the two warring parties; and at the end of the "Whiskey Wars," Capone had gained complete control of all the crime syndicates in the entire city of Chicago.

Chapter Twelve

The Clean Up

Almost everybody in the city of Chicago was delighted over the news of the purported peace treaty between the two warring bootlegging parties; excepting, perhaps, for the detectives in the homicide division who now had dozens of unsolved murders on the books. What with the twenty-seven additional murders which had been committed during the past several weeks of turf warfare, and then added to the five unsolved murders they already had on the books from the St. Valentine's Day Massacre, it was turning into a real nightmare for the Chicago Police Department.

Then too, as a direct result of the sudden rash of bombings and shootings within the city limits of Chicago, the homicide detectives had to be put on overtime pay. Then not so unexpectedly, the Cook County Coroner's Office was forced to ask for additional help from the surrounding Illinois counties.

22
CHICAGO POLICE
DETECTIVE SERGT.
URBS IN HORTO

Chapter Thirteen

The Evidence

In due course, Janice Vincente eventually arrived back home at her parent's house in Iowa; and also just as luckily she was still in one piece. On the other hand, though, Charles Vincente had virtually disappeared from sight. This then led many of the old-time veterans on the Chicago Police Department to believe that Vincente was most likely already dead and buried somewhere out in the Cook County countryside; and therefore, they'd written him off as another probable victim of the gang wars.

But being that Janice was physically removed from the city of Chicago by well over two hundred miles, she found that both her bodily and mental health conditions had begun to steadily improve; she was, however, still more than a little concerned about her own personal safety.

Then after arriving safely back home in Iowa, Janice had very quickly learned that Detective Sergeant James Morris of the Chicago Police Department had called specifically for her while she was still enroute from Chicago; and so she immediately returned the detective's phone call just so she could describe to him in detail just exactly what types of evidence that she had in her possession against her husband, Charles Vincente.

Unfortunately though, James was out of the office and was unavailable on the evening that Janice had made the initial phone call; but of course, she was told that the detective would return her phone call just as quickly as possible. Then once the two of them were connected by telephone, Janice just naturally agreed to honor his request by mailing the incriminating documents directly to the proper police station in Chicago.

Then notwithstanding the passage of a few more days' time, James was extremely grateful to have finally received the stacks of incriminating paperwork from Janice: but then after having read only a few pages of the hodgepodge of evidence he soon realized that some of the information included therein was so sensitive in nature that it could only be shared with certain members of the Chicago Police Department; and that was simply because of the fact that a few of the names mentioned in the evidence package were those of people who currently held high-ranking public offices in the hierarchy of Chicago's City Government.

Chapter Fourteen

Words That Should Never
Be Spoken Aloud

Just as James and his partner had done on many other previous occasions during similar such gang wars, the two detectives once again vowed that they would make a determined effort to pick up as many of Capone's known associates as they possibly could. Regrettably though, they quickly discovered that the majority of the bootleggers were still in hiding.

In the meantime, however, the speakeasies in the city Chicago were beginning to run dangerously low on liquor: and therefore, the bootleggers had only one option left open to them; they would have to return to work, and soon. In due time, the majority of the bootleggers did return to their jobs of manufacturing and distributing the beer and the liquor to their customers; and so naturally, the two detectives were in a much better position to locate at least a few of the gangsters.

Accordingly, then, anytime that they were successful in finding at least one of the murderous bootlegging gangsters, they more often than not interrogated them in one of the darkened basements of a police station, where as a rule, they sometimes resorted in using the old proverbial blackjack and rubber hose on them in order to extract the information that they required; it was just a sign of the times.

Nevertheless, the next few days yielded nothing but fruitless effort on the part of the two detectives; but then once James had found the time to more thoroughly study the secretly obtained handwritten copies of Vincente's old telephone conversations he was taken aback when one of the names on a scrap of paper practically jumped off the page at him. So naturally, James immediately called Janice back to ask her what she knew about that one particular individual.

"Janice this is Detective Sergeant Morris of the Chicago Police Department and I just called to personally thank you for sending me the information and evidence package on Charles Vincente; and oh by the way, as I was reading through your notes I couldn't help but notice that you'd circled one person's name several times; and so naturally, I just wondered if your husband had ever talked to you about that one particular individual," James said.

"Well to tell you the truth Sergeant Morris I'd circled that name several times because it was only the second time in the entire four years that I lived with Charles that I'd ever heard him speak that politely to anybody else over the telephone," Janice said.

"So then does that mean that you did recognize the name and the voice?" James asked.

"Well Sergeant Morris it wasn't so much that I recognized the voice, but the only other time I ever heard Charles speak that softly to anybody else was when he was on the telephone with Al Capone," Janice said.

"Is it possible then that your husband was talking to Al Capone on the days that you circled that particular name?" Morris asked.

"No sir, Sergeant Morris, I don't believe so, because when Charles was on the telephone with Mr. Capone he always used the word boss: then too, the only other time I ever heard Charles speak that politely with anyone else was when he was on the phone with the person whose name I'd circled several times; and looking back, I now realize that I took note of those conversations because of the way Charles kept repeating the words, Sir and your Honor," Janice said.

After thanking Janice for her help, James then very unhappily hung up the telephone.

22
CHICAGO POLICE
DETECTIVE SERGT.
URBS IN HORTO

Chapter Fifteen

A Bitter Pill to Swallow

The very next thing that James had to attend to was to check in with his Lieutenant and Captain in order to advise them of his intentions regarding the evidence that he now had against Vincente; and then once he'd completed that task James telephoned the Chief of Detectives to not only inform him of the latest developments concerning the St. Valentine's Day Massacre, but also to advise him of the hand written evidence that Janice had furnished.

Per his request, James was immediately granted an appointment with the Chief of Detectives; and as he was slowing working his way through traffic en route to the main police headquarters building, James instinctively began to mentally review his notes.

By then, James was already more than a little convinced that he finally understood where most of the missing pieces of the puzzle lay; and he also firmly believed that the answers to the riddle stemmed back to that one particular day when he and his partner were conducting one of their more vigorous interrogations of a suspect when the detainee suddenly began ranting and raving like a madman.

"Look youse guys: I'm just a street soldier here, alright; and besides, you coppers know damn well where the orders come from so why in the hell are you messing with me?" the mobster said.

"Because we know you work for Al Capone, that's why" James said.

"Well if you want to know anything else about what's going on in the city of Chicago why don't you just go ask the mayor himself," the hoodlum said.

Ultimately, James found himself sitting in the Chief of Detective's office where he had an excellent chance to make his case. Then once the chief had had a chance to more fully review the Vincente papers and the secretly copied telephone conversations which had been furnished by Janice, he told James that he was going to ask him for his read on the situation; but first, the chief quoted an old English proverb which stated, "Adversity is the Trial of Courage."

"Chicago doesn't need another trial of an elected public official: if you get my drift," the chief said.

"I wholeheartedly agree with you chief," James said.

"Detective Sergeant Morris how would you like to be promoted to the rank of Detective Lieutenant?" the chief said. Of course, James had only to meditate on that statement for a moment or so since it was fairly obvious where the conversation was headed.

"And I should do what with this evidence?" James said.

"Detective Lieutenant Morris you should take this evidence to the grave with you; and of course that means that the names of the people who allowed the St. Valentine's Day Massacre to happen must never be made public," the chief said.

And as unfortunate as it may be, in those days that was just business as usual.

THE DUMPSTER

CHAPTER ONE

TO SERVE

By serving in the U. S. Military during the Korean Conflict Peter Morris automatically became eligible for the G. I. Bill. So immediately following his honorable discharge from the army he decided to take advantage of the government's generous offer by attending the University of Illinois; Chicago. Then upon graduation, there was never any doubt in Peter's mind as to what he would with the rest of his life since it was a foregone conclusion that he would follow in his father's footsteps by becoming a member of the Chicago Police Department.

Peter's father, Detective Lieutenant James Morris, had enjoyed a memorable career in law enforcement while serving on the Chicago Police Department; and James was especially proud of the role that he'd played as the lead detective on the infamous St. Valentine Day's Massacre that took place in the year of nineteen hundred and twenty-nine.

Then of course, once Peter had been accepted as a member of the Chicago Police Department, he would still be obligated to attend the Illinois Police Academy where he would have to undergo several months of intensive training before he could expect to be assigned to one of the uniform divisions as a probationary patrolman.

Though as time would tell, Peter's hard work ethic while he was in the academy, and then along with, of course, his thorough study of the Police Officer's Uniform Code Books had apparently served him well because after working in the various uniform divisions for only a relatively short period of time he was assigned to the detective division; and his rapid rise up through the ranks of the police department just happened to coincide with the beginnings of one of the most devastating drug epidemics America had seen up to that point in time.

In the end, however, it would become abundantly clear to the people in law enforcement that the country had only experienced the very first stage of what would later evolve into a major drug problem: and in due time, the American drug epidemic would worsen to such a degree that by the end of the twentieth century the use of illegal drugs would not only wreak havoc upon all of the various law enforcement agencies spread across the United States, but the drug scourge would almost completely overwhelm the nation's health and prison systems.

Yet back in the early nineteen fifties the majority of the people who worked in law enforcement were just barely beginning to understand how devastatingly dangerous the use of illegal drugs would eventually become.

Also during the early nineteen fifties, but unbeknownst to the average American, another strange occurrence was beginning to take place; for it was then that a few of the other illegal drugs, such as marijuana and heroin, had already become quite popular with some of the musicians and others who traveled across the country in pursuit of their chosen careers. But then also during those very same years, literally thousands of American Servicemen were about to be introduced to the highly addictive painkilling drug morphine while recuperating from the combat wounds that they'd suffered during the Korean Conflict.

Therefore, and almost certainly as a direct result of our U. S. Servicemen being first introduced to the drug morphine while still in the military, America was about to face another serious societal problem when the U. S. unwittingly loosed those thousands of morphine addicted soldiers back home upon the streets of their hometowns.

Moreover, when those newly addicted ex-servicemen first began arriving back home in the states, they then very quickly discovered that the drug morphine could be easily obtained on the mean streets of the cities where they lived; and also just as regrettably, many of those former U. S. Military Veterans would eventually go on to become severely addicted to that most insidious drug, morphine.

First and foremost, though, the nation's drug laws back in the nineteen fifties were ambiguous and still undefined at best: and as a direct result of those lax drug laws the drug morphine could be easily acquired at practically any U. S. pharmacy; and that same worst case scenario was even more true if a person happened to know someone who worked in the healthcare field. And if the easy availability of that highly addictive drug wasn't bad enough, another strange occurrence was about to take place within the Chicago Police Department itself.

Notwithstanding the seriousness of this unforeseen drug problem, the situation was about to become even more problematic for the old-time police officers when they first began to encounter the newly addicted morphine addicts on the streets of their hometowns, where at first glance, many of the veteran police officers believed that the morphine addicts were insane. However, some of the confusion in the minds of those veteran officers stemmed from the fact that they had not as yet been properly trained on how to deal with this new type of criminal.

Then as soon as the morphine addicted ex-soldiers began to appear on the city streets of Chicago in greater numbers, the police officers who worked their assigned districts on a day to day basis began to see crimes against humanity of the types that they'd only witnessed in combat situations while serving in either the Second World War or the Korean Conflict.

Back in the nineteen fifties, however, homicide detective Peter Morris would have almost certainly been the first to admit that he was still somewhat naïve about how potentially dangerous the drug problem in America would eventually become; and also just as unfortunately, Peter had arrived at the erroneous conclusion that the United States was impervious to something as sinister as having an entire generation addicted to drugs. Besides, as Peter had repeatedly told himself, hadn't America been victorious in both of the World Wars in Europe and Asia, and hadn't we also won a lasting peace in Korea?

Ultimately, however, Peter did begin to wonder if the only other recourse of action left open for the Federal and State Governments would be to make the drug laws more stringent in the hopes that society would see a drastic reduction in the rising numbers of homicides and other violent crimes that were escalating at an alarming rate across this great country of ours.

Tough new drug laws, and or, court ordered drug rehabilitation; would that be the answer to this seemingly unsolvable problem? Peter wondered. Nevertheless, the average American's attitude on the drug habits of a fast growing and sizeable proportion of the general public was about to be radically changed when in the year of nineteen hundred and fifty-five the American Medical Association decided to define alcoholism as a disease. Albeit, their proposition just barely passed through that prestigious organization's membership by only the slimmest of margins; but then too, and also just as unfortunate for the addicts of America, the A. M. A. wouldn't get around to including drug addiction in that definition until the year of nineteen hundred and eighty-seven. Consequently, the person who used illegal drugs in the early nineteen fifties was still considered a criminal.

But be that as it may, and even though Peter was somewhat sympathetic to the plight of the U. S. Servicemen who'd become addicted to the pain killing drug morphine while serving their country, he was still in favor of placing the blame squarely on the shoulders of the addicts where he felt it so rightfully belonged; and Peter also fervently believed that the drug addicts and alcoholics who committed thievery, robbery, and murder in order to support their habits should be imprisoned for their illegal actions.

Then too, along with everything else that was happening in the nineteen fifties, another interesting and historical event was about to take place when the Federal Government decided to sponsor a few of the so-called educational types of films in which the illegal drug marijuana was touted to be a substance that would cause the people who smoked the drug to go insane.

Therefore, and almost certainly as a direct result of the government's anti-marijuana propaganda films, the whole of American society would eventually come to believe that the use of any illegal drugs whatsoever would not only shut down the moral and civilized parts of the user's brains, but that the use of the drugs would almost certainly cause the addicts to commit a whole multitude of violent acts; and then later on, of course, the fears of those early prognosticators would prove to be right on target.

Did America need a war on drugs?, Peter wondered. Although at that point in time his thinking was that if the National Prohibition Act of the nineteen twenties and thirties had failed so miserably in its attempt to stop the average American from drinking alcohol, then how in the world could the Federal Government ever begin to imagine that they could convince the masses of the American populace to stop using illegal drugs by simply showing them a few scary films about the dangers of smoking marijuana.

Chapter Two

A Body with No Name

In the past, hardly anyone had ever complained about the stench coming from the multitudes of dumpsters which are normally found in the rear of the apartment buildings scattered throughout the near North Side of Chicago; and especially since the dumpsters are almost always full of smelly garbage anyway. It's also a well-known fact that the dumpsters don't usually get emptied for three full days during national holidays. However, on one seemingly normal and unparticular 4th of July, with the temperature hovering in the middle nineties, the Chicago Police were called to a middle-income neighborhood on the near North Side of town to investigate an unusually strong order that supposedly was coming from a trash dumpster.

Consequently, then, on that very hot and humid day in the month of July while our nation was celebrating its birthday, a police car was dispatched to the complainant's address where the first officers on the scene were dutifully met by a sweet little old lady who insisted that they do something about the noxious odor that was emanating from the dumpsters in the rear of her apartment building complex. In the female's official complaint she was quoted as saying, "That earlier that morning when she'd tried to place her garbage in the dumpster, her poodle had run away from the foul-smelling air, as indeed had she."

So then primarily because of the lady's firmness of resolve for the officers to further investigate her complaint, they had no other recourse but to look inside the dumpster where to their surprise they found a nude and bloody female human body which lay in plain view atop the bagged garbage. The crime scene was then immediately secured while the uniformed officers waited for the homicide detectives to arrive. Detectives Peter Morris and Don Combs of the Chicago Police Department's Homicide Division caught the case.

"Is it hot enough for you today detective Morris?" A uniformed officer said.

"It doesn't get much better than this, does it officer Scapelli?" Peter said.

"You know it kind of reminds me of what Mark Twain once said," "Everybody talks about the weather but nobody does anything about it," the uniformed officer said.

But then after completing their own preliminary investigation, the two detectives turned the crime scene over to the medical examiner; and in due time, the victim's body was transported to the Cook County Morgue where an autopsy would be performed.

Also later on that same morning, but only after first making sure that the crime scene was properly secured and manned, Peter and Don made their way over to the city morgue where they were to learn that not only had their homicide victim been stabbed repeatedly in the upper part of the torso, but that any one of the numerous stab wounds could have caused her death. Then too, the M. E. told the two detectives that there wouldn't be any more information available until after the autopsy had been performed.

But then being that they were at the morgue anyway, Peter and Don decided to wait around for a little while longer just so they could obtain a copy of their victim's fingerprints which would then be compared to the myriad numbers of prints already on file in the police department's records division.

Unfortunately for the two detectives, however, the technicians in the crime lab were unable to match their victim's fingerprints to any name that they had listed in their local I. D. system. This then meant, of course, that the twenty to twenty-five year old white female homicide victim had never before been arrested; or at least she'd never been arrested in the city of Chicago.

Therefore, and much to their dismay, the two detectives were left with a victim who not only had never been fingerprinted, but the Missing Persons Bureau had also failed to link the victim's body size, approximate age, and hair coloring to any female who'd recently been reported missing from the Chicago area; and which then meant that the young female homicide victim would have to be officially listed as another Jane Doe.

Back in the nineteen fifties when the authorities found themselves in possession of a John or a Jane Doe, or even if police had a prime suspect in a criminal matter, a viable set of fingerprints would have had to have been sent to the F. B. I. Headquarters in Washington, D.C. Although from his own personal experiences Peter knew that a procedure of that type could take up two or three weeks, or even longer, before they could expect to hear from the Feds.

Moreover, just having to wait around for weeks on end to receive the results of a fingerprint inquiry from the F. B. I. has always been problematic for any homicide detective; and therefore, it's of the upmost importance for homicide investigators to be able to identify the victim just as quickly as possible. Thus, as any homicide investigator will readily tell you, just the act of having the victim's name is an indispensable tool with which a detective will heavily depend upon; and especially since the first forty-eight hours immediately following a murder are always the most critical times when it comes to solving a case of homicide.

Then as a result of their slow start on their latest Jane Doe case, and also being that Peter and Don were already more than a little disappointed with their inability to identify their victim, they decided that wisest thing for them to do would be to revisit the dumpster site where the victim's body was found just so they could get a better feel for the surroundings.

Generally speaking, anytime that Peter was assigned to a brand new case of homicide he more often than not felt that it's much more difficult for a homicide investigator to be able to fully grasp the entire picture at a fresh crime scene until later on when all of the medical technicians and the uniformed police officers have retired from the scene.

So fortunately for Peter and Don, by the time that they were able to make their way back to the dumpster site most of the uniformed police officers, and even the Crime Scene Investigators, had left the area. In their place, however, there were several other teams of detectives that were already in the process of canvassing the people who lived in the nearby apartment complexes. Peter and Don immediately joined the other teams of detectives in hopes of talking to some of the people in the neighborhood who'd not been at home earlier in the day when the police officers had first knocked on their doors.

Chapter Three

The Un-Total Picture

As a child growing up in the city of Chicago, Peter Morris had accompanied his father on many of those Saturday morning trips to the various police stations in the downtown area. However, it wasn't until much later on in life when Peter became more fully aware of the magnificently carved stone representations of the mythical gargoyles and the other animals which are occasionally featured upon the upper facades and the friezes of some of the older buildings.

So when Peter gets his first look at a present-day crime scene, he is sometimes reminded of those Saturday morning trips to the downtown districts with his father when he'd first failed to notice the stone carvings on the fronts of some of those ancient buildings.

So primarily because of that one learning experience from the far distant past, Peter has since taught himself to take a much closer look at the minor details of a new case which are almost always present at the scene of a homicide; and Peter is also ever mindful to take a harder look at the facts of a new case even when they don't appear to represent what they actually may be.

At this stage in his career, however, Peter was considered by his peers to be a notably experienced and well-seasoned homicide investigator; but that's not to say that there haven't been times in the past when he'd found it very difficult to grasp the total meaning of both the physical and emotional clues which are sometimes left behind at the scene of a crime.

Then too, whenever Peter is in the midst of investigating a brand new case of homicide he will occasionally run across a few facts which might make him wonder if perhaps his inability to fully understand the true meaning of a crime scene might be comparable to the age-old psychological challenge of not being able to see the forest for the trees.

However, that's not to say that Peter faces anymore challenges than any of the other homicide investigators in his squad: for as a rule, he's more often than not able to identify the killer or killers by simply working backwards through the members of the victim's family and their closets friends and associates; and therefore, his close ratio percentage on the cases he works is usually higher than anybody else's in the squad. Even so, Peter is well aware of the fact that approximately one third of all the reported homicide cases in the United States will eventually end up going cold.

Still, when Peter is in the middle of attempting to solve a case of homicide there are times when he feels as though he might as well be staring at one of those ultramodern artist innovations which are sometimes found in magazine ads. In those ads, if a person were to focus on a picture of a glass of liquor and ice cubes long enough, then they might even begin to imagine that they are viewing images of nude human figures on the insides of the ice cubes and the bubbles of the liquid.

So regardless of the fact that Peter is known to be an experienced homicide investigator, there are times when the clues at a crime scene can be just as confusing to him as those whiskey ads are to the ordinary person's mind. Then again, that's not to say that the detectives are actually looking for nude images or anything like that, but when homicide investigators continue to focus on a murder scene for a long period of time then it can be very difficult for them to be able to encompass the total picture.

DETECTIVE
CHICAGO POLICE
20588

Chapter Four

A distorted image

And even though Peter Morris has been fairly successful in the solving of a goodly number of the homicide cases that he's worked in the past, he would still be the first to admit that there are parts of the human psyche' that continue to baffle him; and therefore, when he begins working on a new case of homicide he almost always tries to first explore the psychological aspects of each new assignment by attempting to think the thoughts of the yet unknown killer or killers.

Thus by employing his own methods of reasoning and psychology to the latest Jane Doe case, Peter began surveying the approaches to the dumpster from every conceivable angle: and which not only included the accesses from the street and the rear doors of the adjacent apartment buildings but he decided to also include the access to the nearby river that would have been available to the killer as well. Even so, Peter couldn't help but wonder why the killer had chosen to place the victim's body in the frequently used dumpster instead of trying to hide the body in one of the area's other less conspicuous places.

"Let me ask you something Don: if you were the killer where would you have placed the body?" Peter said.

"Well Peter, I'm not quite sure: although I think I might have hidden the body over there behind that shed on the other side of the EL Train tracks since the shed is partially hidden from view by those piss-elms and pussy-willow trees; then again, I might have just dumped the body in the water since the river isn't really that away from the dumpster anyway," Don said, in his Southern tongue.

"That's exactly what I was thinking; so to me, that means just two things. One of which is that the killer wasn't thinking any too clearly; and then secondly, it might just mean that someone wanted the body to be found. More importantly, though, if the second scenario turns out to be the case then we can be rest assured that the killer will be dumping more bodies in and around the city of Chicago," Peter said.

Chapter Five

A Journalistic View

Then finally, when the long hard day at the dumpster site and the morgue was mercifully over and done with, Peter and his wife Lou Ann were enjoying themselves by relaxing at their kitchen table as they listened to a radio broadcast of a Chicago Cub's baseball game. Once again, Peter was secretly hoping for another Chicago Cub's World Series Championship; though at that point in time the Cubs hadn't won the World Series of baseball since the year of nineteen hundred and eight. Although the Cubs had at least managed to make it into the nineteen hundred and forty-five World Series; and which then had prompted Peter to remember that it was also the very same year that the hostilities of World War Two had finally ended.

Even so, the avid sports fans of Chicago were once again hoping and praying that their beloved Cubbies would at least have a winning season that year. Then again, they usually said the same thing every year; until, that is, when the playoffs rolled around for that's generally when the Cubs always managed to run out of gas, Peter mused to himself.

Then at the conclusion of the radio broadcast of the Cub's baseball game, and also being that he was a creature of habit, Peter automatically turned on the television set just so he could watch the late evening news. Though at the very beginning of the newscast Peter was absolutely flabbergasted when a local T. V. anchorperson began the broadcast by describing in the most vivid and grisly details some of the facts surrounding a frightful and gruesome murder which had just taken place on the near North Side of Chicago; but what had disturbed Peter the most was the fact that the T. V. announcer seemed to be in possession of a few details of the case which had not been released to the general public.

In addition to stating that the poor murdered girl whose nude body was found in a dumpster on the North Side of town had been injected with the painkilling drug morphine, the T. V. announcer went on to say that in his opinion the young female victim had most likely been killed by another, "Dope Fiend."

When thankfully, it was time for the anchorperson's evening editorial comments, he concluded his critique of the city's latest murder by advising everybody on the near North Side of town to not only remember to lock their doors and windows before retiring for the evening, but that they should also remain even more cautious and alert; it was sensationalistic journalism at its worst, Peter thought.

Chapter Six

Dead Ends and Drugs

The next morning came early for Peter and Don: and after first signing in on the duty board in the squad room they then hurriedly checked in with their boss, Lieutenant Aaron Tabor, just to keep him up to date on the progress of their latest Jane Doe case.

Of course both Peter and Don were well aware of the fact their relationship with their superior officer had just recently been on the decline; but they also knew that the friction in the squad room was primarily caused by their lack of progress on the Jane Doe case that they were presently working.

But since there was still more important work awaiting them out there on the streets, they hurriedly made their way out of the stationhouse and began to slowly work their way through traffic towards the Cook County Morgue where they hoped to ascertain the results of the autopsy on their latest Jane Doe. Though on their way over to the morgue they were still trying desperately to determine how the facts of their dumpster case had leaked so quickly to the press.

At first, Don had thought that it might have been one of the emergency medical technicians at the crime scene who'd most inappropriately released a few of the details of their case to the press. Of course they also both knew that there was always a good possibility that one of Chicago's finest had inadvertently talked to someone they shouldn't have after first imbibing too many pints of ale at one of their favorite watering holes.

Then after arriving back at the morgue, Peter and Don headed straight for the medical examiner's office where they were to learn that a good many of the wounds on their Jane doe's body had been inflicted post-mortem, or after she was already dead; but to their big surprise they discovered that their victim had actually died as a direct result of an overdose of the drug morphine. This latest finding by the medical team was somewhat perplexing to the two detectives; and especially since the subsequent autopsy and lab tests had proved that their Jane Doe homicide victim wasn't even an addict.

So by then, Peter and Don were more than a little confused by the enormity of it all and especially since the M. E. had just informed them that their victim's cause of death was to be listed as a drug overdose. So when Peter asked the M. E. just how she knew for certain that the victim wasn't an addict, the doctor replied that the answer was really quite simple and then stated that the lab tests they'd performed on their Jane Doe had shown that there was no significant damage to the liver resulting from alcohol or any other kind of drug abuse.

The M. E. then stated further that she'd also conducted another scientific test by viewing a strand of the victim's hair under a microscope which she said was another way by which the medical technicians could prove or disprove whether an individual was a chronic user of drugs. Then too, Peter and Don weren't all that surprised when the M. E. told them that not only had their Jane Doe previously given birth to at least one child, but that she was several months pregnant at the time of her death.

And even though Peter still had a hundred unrequited questions for the good doctor, his thoughts were interrupted by one of the lab technicians who informed him that Lieutenant Tabor had just called and had left orders for them to return at once to the stationhouse for an emergency squad meeting.

Then just as soon as all of the members of the squad were present and accounted for, Lieutenant Tabor began the early morning meeting by reading an article from one of the local newspapers. It was apparent that not only had the T. V. anchor person from the previous evening been tipped off by an insider, but it was also fairly obvious to everybody in the squad room that the writer of that particular newspaper account was in possession of some of the unrevealed facts concerning the morphine murder of the young woman whose lifeless body had been abandoned in the dumpster.

Hence, at the conclusion of his speech, which was unusually long for him, Lieutenant Tabor stated that in his opinion thc writer of this latest newspaper story had grossly overestimated the seriousness of the drug situation in their fair city by claiming that the city of Chicago was experiencing such an influx of illegal drugs and addicts that the entire police department was about to be completely overwhelmed by the total consequences of it all.

Though as a rule, Lieutenant Tabor was considered by most to be a well centered and levelheaded man; and therefore, a statement such as the one that he'd just issued came as a total surprise to almost everybody at the meeting. Yet on that particular morning the lieutenant appeared to be more than a little annoyed by what he considered to be an inaccurate account of the local situation; and which then must have led him to state even further that in his opinion the journalist who'd written that highly inflammatory newspaper editorial had greatly over exaggerated the extinct of the illegal drug use in the city of Chicago.

Though without a doubt, most of the detectives who were in attendance at that early morning meeting were more than a little taken aback by Lieutenant Tabor's seemingly harsh words. For as a rule, it certainly wasn't customary for him to voice his opinion on anything that was being reported in the local media. On that particular morning, however, Lieutenant Tabor very emphatically expressed his personal views on the subject of journalism by repeating to the squad members what he'd repeatedly told them and that was not only was he somewhat skeptical of anything that he reads in the newspapers, but that he also believes only about half of what he sees with his own two eyes.

Then after stating that the Chief of the Chicago Police Department had ordered the following statement concerning mandatory drug education to be read in every district, the lieutenant said that he had no other recourse then but to obey.

"Ladies and gentlemen: our chief has just issued a statement that he wishes to be read at every roll-call in every police station in the city of Chicago; and it reads as follows," the lieutenant said.

"Notwithstanding the age-old tradition of allowing our Vice and Narcotics Division to continue to have the main responsibility of controlling the use of, and the sale of illegal drugs in our community, from this time forward every Chicago Police Officer is hereby ordered to become more knowledgeable about the drug problem that is currently sweeping across this great country of ours and is fast becoming a national crisis. Therefore, all members of the Chicago police Department will hereby be required to attend additional training classes in order for us to not only become more fully aware of the latest drug laws, but that we should also strive to become more knowledgeable of the potential dangers which are closely associated with the scourge of drug addiction," the lieutenant said, quoting the chief.

To say the least, Peter was more than a little impressed by the length of, and also by the substance of the lieutenant's early morning emergency meeting; and particularly since Lieutenant Tabor's squad meetings were usually more parsimonious and short lived at best. Then again, Peter was also well aware of the fact that lieutenant Tabor didn't necessarily enjoy speaking in front of large groups of people.

Consequently, then, when the early morning emergency meeting was finally over and done with, it seemed as if everybody in the squad had a different opinion on how best to proceed with their own personal education of the escalating drug problem.

"I happen to know of a brand new drug rehab clinic that has just recently opened its doors for business; and therefore, it might just be the best place for us to start looking for answers," Don said.

"I'll have to admit that what little I know about drug addiction is what they taught us at those seminars that I attended awhile back at the Illinois Police Academy. But to tell you the truth, Don, I wholeheartedly agree with the chief in as much as that everybody on the force needs to be better informed about the inherent dangers of the current drug problem. Then too, our continued homication on the subject will definitely become more important to us later on if the crime rate continues to escalate; and which is exactly what every knowledgeable person in the city of Chicago expects to happen," Peter said.

The drug and alcohol rehabilitation center that Don had in mind to visit was conveniently located in a suburb to the west of Chicago; and then once they were on the clinic's grounds, the two detectives were more than a little impressed with the beautiful architecture of the institute's buildings which they thought looked more like a college campus than what they'd envisioned a drug rehab facility would look like. However, their hopes of obtaining any useful information on the issue of drug addiction were soon dashed when the director explained to them that the rules concerning the Federal Rights of Privacy Laws had been put into place to protect the rights of the patients; this then meant, of course, that the patient's names and the types of their addictions were deemed confidential.

And so with no other urgent plans, the next thing on Peter and Don's list of things to do that day was to visit one of the local Veterans Affairs Clinics. Unfortunately, though, the administrator at the V. A. Clinic only confirmed what they'd previously been told about the patient's rights of privacy laws.

In the last analysis, however, Peter could, of course, see the need for a patient in a hospital, or even a person in a rehab clinic, to be able to expect a certain amount of privacy concerning their medical conditions; but by then, the two detectives were already more than a little disappointed with their lack of progress on the "Dumpster Case," as it was officially known throughout the squad.

Then notwithstanding the seemingly hopelessness of the situation at hand, and then too, by feeling as if they had no other avenues open to them, Peter and don decided to seek council from the detectives in the Vice and Narcotics Division. Regrettably, though, Peter and Don were once again disappointed when the Norco dicks told them that the majority of the drug cases that they were then working were those involving the other types of illegal drugs such as heroin and marijuana and not the drug morphine.

So then following their luckless interview with the dicks in vice, it was quite understandable that Peter was feeling even more discouraged with their lack of progress on their latest homicide case. Even so, Peter had been on the job long enough to know that when something jumps off the radar screen then a good cop has no other alternative but to follow his nose to its final conclusion. For at that point in time Peter believed with all his heart that they were either chasing a Korean Era War Veteran, or else a morphine addicted musician, or just possibly a combination of the two.

Besides, as Peter kept telling himself, it's always sounder to listen to someone like the great Roman orator Cicero who once said, "Nobody can give you better advice than yourself."

Chapter Seven

Routine detective work

In the meantime, Peter and Don were forced to squander the next several days by chasing down old fruitless and dead-end leads. Though in time they were finally able to gain Lieutenant Tabor's permission to place their Jane Doe's morgue photograph in the local newspapers.

Of course everybody on the force already knew that publicity is always their best tool when it comes to identifying a John or a Jane Doe; and therefore, Peter wasn't any too surprised when they received a phone call from a waitress who purportedly worked at a tavern that was located on the near North Side of town.

Hence, as soon as the call from the waitress was transferred to his desk, Peter just naturally became very interested in what the woman had to say; and especially when the caller stated that the image in the morgue photo reminded her of a girl that she used to work with.

Then as quickly as they could, Peter and Don signed out of the squad room and then hurriedly drove over to the bar where the waitress supposedly worked. Then once they were in the general area of the bar, Peter just happened to remember a homicide case that he'd previously worked in that very same district. And if memory served him, that particular part of town consisted mainly of a residential area which included approximately ten or twelve square blocks of mostly older style townhouses and duplexes; but then he also remembered that there was semi-industrial area located nearby which just happened to include a large number of bars and restaurants.

Thus as luck would have it, the woman who'd made the initial phone call to the stationhouse was just coming on duty when the detectives arrived; and consequently, it was beginning to look as if their recent string of good luck was about to continue. Furthermore, once the waitress had the time to more fully view the morgue photo of their Jane Doe she stated that if it was the same girl that she used to work with then her name would either be Sandy Brown or Bronson. The waitress then added that the confusion surrounding the girl's surname stemmed from the fact that the girl she'd known as Sandy had used several different last names while serving her customers.

Nonetheless, when the bartender was shown the very same photo of the dumpster case victim, he too identified the woman in the photo as being the same woman he'd known as Sandy Burton: but then added that Sandy had worked at the bar for only a brief period of time before missing a couple of shifts; and also that she'd failed to return to work again even though he was still holding a paycheck for her. Unfortunately, though, when the detectives asked the bartender for Sandy's home address he replied by saying that he couldn't seem to find her file in his employee's record book.

They say that the more things change the more they stay the same: but then after having been a homicide investigator for the past several years Peter had learned the hard way that the only dumb questions are the ones that you don't ask. And since Peter was already more than a little aggravated with the manager of the bar for the sloppy way in which he kept the employee's record books, he couldn't help but to query the two employees as to why they hadn't reported the girl missing after she'd failed to show up for work.

At first, the waitress seemed to be a little put off by Peter's blunt style of questioning: but then once she'd had the chance to calm down a bit she stated that she really hadn't thought that it was any of her business to report the girl missing; and particularly since it was obvious that Sandy was one of those kinds of girls who always come and go anyway.

Amazingly, though, while the waitress was standing there idly aside, first with her hands on her hips, but then also with her body cocked slightly to one side, she told the detectives that, "Sandy had a bad attitude about herself;" but more importantly she said that, "Sandy just wasn't the responsible type of worker like she was." And then as if to prove her point to Peter and Don, she said that not only had she worked at the same bar for the past ten years, but that she'd done so without ever missing a single day's work.

It was understandable that Peter and Don were grateful for the chance to get away from the two nuts in the bar, but then as soon as they were on the outside Peter remembered something that his father had told him about human nature; and that simply was that people tend to shop, eat out, and live close by to where they work. So then by continuing with that single premise of thought Peter could only assume that Sandy lived somewhere in the immediate surrounding area of the bar.

Therefore, the detectives decided to only canvass the bars and the restaurants that were located in the ten square block area surrounding the bar where they believed Sandy Burton had previously worked. And after several more hours of hard work, they luckily ran across a bartender who said that a girl by the name of Sandy had worked for him in the not too far distant past.

Indeed, Lady Luck must have been smiling down on the two detectives that day for no sooner had the bartender had a chance to take a better look at the morgue photo then he said that the girl in the picture was definitely the same woman that he knew as Sandy Burton.

Unfortunately, though, when Peter asked for Sandy's home address the bartender stated that he was unable to find her paperwork in the cigar boxful of receipts and papers that he apparently used for his filing system.

So even though the two detectives still didn't have a verifiable home address for their dumpster case victim, they were at least somewhat grateful to have finally come up with a name that could they append to the photo in the murder book instead of having to always refer to their victim as a Jane Doe.

Then notwithstanding all of the hard work and the man-hours that they'd already put into the dumpster case, Peter and Don were about to once again be mildly disappointed when they were unable to find Sandy Burton's name listed anywhere in the Record's Division at the stationhouse, or even in the Chicago telephone book; and as if to add more insult to injury they learned that there were literally dozens of Burtons listed in the Chicago City Directory. However, after narrowing down the long list of names and addresses from the directory to the people who lived in that specific ten square block area surrounding the bar where Sandy had once worked, they soon discovered that there were only a handful of names and street addresses that actually qualified.

More importantly, though, Peter and Don were in possession of a morgue photo of their homicide victim whom they believed to be a woman named Sandy Burton;

and so instead of calling up all of the people named Burton on the telephone, they decided to visit each and every one of the addresses in person.

Of course anytime that Pater and Don found themselves involved in one of those nitty-gritty, gum-shoe type of homicide cases like the one that they were presently working, they were certainly well aware of the fact that just the act of solving any case of homicide will almost invariably involve a lot of hard work and good luck; that said, one can always hope for an early success. On the other hand, though, they didn't really expect to be fortunate enough to locate any of Sandy's relatives on the very first try.

On the other hand, though, their chances for an early success seemed to improve somewhat when a middle-aged woman with two small children hanging onto her apron strings answered the door at the third residence on their list.

At first, the lady at the door had trouble understanding what the detectives were trying to say: but then once she'd quieted the two crying children she was in a much better way to more fully understand the true nature of their visit; and only then did the woman finally acknowledge that not only did she have a daughter by the name of Sandy, but that her daughter was the mother of the two small children who were standing before them.

"Mrs. Burton did your daughter ever work at the Night Spot Tavern?" Peter said.

"Why yes, I believe she did work there for a short period of time. But you see she quit that job awhile back when she met a musician by the name of Frank, who by the way, just recently went back on the road again and unfortunately, this time he took Sandy along with him;

and as you can plainly see, that's why I am now babysitting her two young children," Mrs. Burton said.

"Did Sandy ever tell you Frank's last name, or where he lived?" Peter said.

"No sir: as a matter of fact she didn't; and you know that's the strangest part of this whole situation because about a week ago when Sandy dropped off the kids she promised that she would come by the house on the following morning to give me the telephone numbers of the motels where she and Frank would be staying while they were out of town. Unfortunately, though, she hasn't returned home yet: and consequently, I really don't have any way to get in touch with her; and as you can well imagine I've been going out of my mind with worry ever since she left town," Mrs. Burton said.

And even though Peter had not as yet shown the lady his copy of Sandy's morgue photo, he still somehow knew that Mrs. Burton was indeed the mother of the slain young woman whose body had just recently been found in the dumpster. Therefore, the next task Peter would be asked to perform is undoubtedly one of the most difficult parts of police work that an officer ever has to deal with; and that simply has to do with notifying the next of kin about the death of a loved one.

Without a doubt, Peter's obligation to duty has always been first and foremost in his mind; then again, he knew full well that it wasn't the right time and place to ask the lady to identify the woman in the morgue photo. For at that point in time Peter main concern was for the consideration of the mother's feelings and so he decided that the best place for that conversation to take place would be at the stationhouse; that is, of course, if Mrs. Burton could find someone to watch the children for a few hours.

Of course if Mrs. Burton really was the mother of the slain young woman named Sandy, then the detectives would be obligated to ask her to accompany them to the city morgue where she would be asked to make an official I. D.

What is more, and as callous as it may seem, if it did turn out that Mrs. Burton was the mother of the recently murdered young woman named Sandy then the two detectives and the coroner would be obligated to ask her to claim her daughter's body; and which in turn would get the county off the hook for the cost of the burial expenses.

Chapter Eight

The list narrows

As a rule, law enforcement officers are hardly ever surprised by the stupidity of the average criminal. All the same, within only a few short days after having made the official I. D. of her daughter at the coroner's office Peter was ecstatic when Mrs. Burton telephoned him at the stationhouse to report that she'd just gotten a letter in the mail in which the writer had stated that not only had Sandy mislead him, but that she deserved everything that'd happened to her.

Of course Peter was immensely pleased with the prospect of finally having some hard evidence against the elusive man named Frank, who he and Don were fervently hoping that he would be the composure of the aforementioned letter; and so naturally, the two detectives then hurriedly then drove over to the Burton residence so that they could personally take charge of the letter. But as soon as they had the envelope in their possession, then their only thought was to quickly deliver that crucial piece of evidence to the police lab where it could be checked for fingerprints.

Regrettably, though, the technicians at the crime lab were unable to retrieve any latent fingerprints from the envelope or the letter itself; and so it was beginning to look as if it was going to be a very difficult matter just to locate Sandy's alleged boyfriend.

Although from past experiences Peter knew full well that police investigators are routinely surprised with new twist and turns while investigating any case of homicide: it simply goes along with the territory; and so it definitely wasn't anything new to him. However, Peter had been on the job long enough to know that when searching for information in the present that he could almost always find the answers he was looking for by taking a closer look at the past.

And even though the modern-day conventional wisdom says that we may glance at the past but that we shouldn't stare, the true meaning of that old adage was definitely not intended for homicide detectives. Accordingly, then, while going back through the Sandy Burton murder book, Peter just happened to come across a note that he'd made that pertained specifically to an earlier interview that he and Don had conducted with Sandy's ex-husband. And even though they'd already investigated the young man named Michael Wade and they'd found no hint of a drug problem, or any other types of arrest on his police record, they decided to return to the body shop where the ex-husband worked anyway just in case the man might be able to shed some further light on the mysterious man named Frank.

In their chosen profession of law enforcement, Peter and Don were used to dealing primarily with the criminal element, therefore, whenever they happened across a halfway normal person such as Michael Wade they sometimes allowed themselves to enjoy a little levity.

"The ex-husband pays his child support on time and he even goes to church on Sundays," Don said.

"This guy's so squeaky clean about the only thing we'll ever be able to pin on him would be the time he put a light in his father's chicken coop so that the rooster would crow at all hours of the day and night," Peter said.

Yet upon arrival at the body shop where the ex-husband was known to be employed, Peter and Don would learn that even though Sandy's ex-husband seemed to be genuinely upset over the death of his children's mother, he also readily admitted to the fact that not only had he just recently filed papers with family court in hopes of gaining full custody of their two young children, but that he'd filed those court papers even well before he'd learned of his ex-wife's death. Moreover, Mike further explained his decision to the two detectives by saying that he felt as though he'd been forced to file those full-custody papers in order to keep his two children away from the strange and unstable new men in Sandy's life,

And even though the detectives had not as yet uncovered any previous criminal history against the ex-husband, Michael Wade, Peter still had to wonder if a statement such as the one just made by him could be construed as a motive for murder.

Yet, when the two detectives finally got around to asking the ex-husband what he knew about the mysterious man named Frank who was allegedly involved with his ex-wife, Mike said that he didn't personally know anybody by the name of Frank; but he did, however, acknowledge that Sandy had once bragged to him about having a new boyfriend whom she said knew how to make big money. But then as Mike went on to say, "Sandy had never gotten around to telling much of anything else about the new man in her life or even how the new boyfriend had made all of that money.

Chapter Nine

Similar Homicides

Then immediately following their latest interview with the ex-husband, Peter and Don decided to head on back to the stationhouse where they were about to learn that the lifeless body of yet another young woman had just been discovered in their district. And in addition to the fact that this was the second homicide of a young female to take place in their sector within only a short period of time, the two detectives would become even more interested in the new case when they discovered that the modus-operandi that was used to dispatch the latest victim was very similar to the M. O. that was used to murder their own victim, Sandy Burton.

Thus being that their district's latest homicide victim was discovered in the same general area where Sandy Burton's body was found, the detectives who'd caught the brand new case of homicide were asked to not only cooperate fully and to work closely with Peter and Don, but they were also told by their lieutenant that they should share any and all of the pertinent information that they happened to come across.

To Peter's way of thinking, about the only real difference he could see in the technique that was used on this latest homicide victim was simply the fact that the victim's body had been dumped in the backseat of an old abandoned parked car instead of being placed in a trash dumpster like the killer had done with Sandy Burton's body.

Therefore, when Peter and Don returned to the city morgue in order to retrieve a copy of the autopsy report on their district's latest homicide victim, they weren't any too surprised when the M. E. informed them that the wounds on the recently murdered young woman's body which had been left in a parked car on the near North Side of town appeared to be very similar to the wounds which had been inflicted on the body of Sandy Burton. Although the real shocker came when the M. E. informed the two detectives that there was enough morphine in the latest victim's system to kill at least two people; so to Peter and Don it was beginning to look as if it could be victim number two and counting. Peter was also thinking that a person wouldn't necessarily have to be a pessimist to imagine that the latest homicide might just be recipe for a disaster for any young female who just happened to be living on the North Side of town.

CHAPTER TEN

THE STAKEOUT

At that point in time things really weren't going all that well for Peter and Don; but within a few days following the discovery of the second female victim in their district another highly unexpected twist to their homicide case was about to rear its ugly head when Mrs. Burton telephoned Peter at the stationhouse to inform him that she'd just received a second letter in the mail. On that particular occasion, however, Mrs. Burton elected to deliver the evidence to the police station in person just so the detectives could review the contents a little more quickly.

Then once Peter had a chance to more thoroughly review the words used in the letter, and then also once he had the time to better understand the true meaning of the composure's style, he told his partner that the author of the letter might have made a grave mistake by warning Sandy's mother not to talk to the police anymore.

It goes without saying that Peter was delighted to have this new information at his disposal and especially since it might just mean that their person of interest was able to observe Mrs. Burton's home at all different hours of the day and night. Of course if that turned out to be the case then perhaps their suspect lived or worked someplace close by to Mrs. Burton's home.

As promised, the second letter was indeed hand delivered to the stationhouse on that very same Friday morning; but then owing to the potential importance of the information contained therein, Peter and Don were able to gain permission from their lieutenant to maintain a stakeout near Mrs. Burton's residence. Yet in addition to gaining permission to watch the mother's house, they were also authorized to photograph all of the vehicles and the persons coming and going through Mrs. Burton's neighborhood.

Regrettably, though, the stakeout of Mrs. Burton's home didn't produce any immediate results during the first full day's work. Nonetheless, Peter and Don were fortunate enough to be able to persuade their lieutenant into allowing them to continue on working throughout the remainder of that Friday evening.

Then precisely at 8:00 O'clock on that dark and rainy Friday evening, a longhaired man in a white van was observed driving slowly past Mrs. Burton's residence; and since Peter and Don were still trying to connect both the longhaired musicians and the ex-servicemen to the drug scene in the city of Chicago, they elected to follow the van to see if perhaps the subject lived or worked somewhere within the ten square block area of the bar where Sandy had previously worked.

Then after following the van closely for only a short period of time, Peter and Don decided that they would attempt to keep their subject under a loose surveillance as the driver of the van continued to make numerous but brief stops at several of the clubs and bars which are located on the near North Side of town.

In due time, however, the longhaired man in the van began driving directly towards the western-most suburbs of Chicago before eventually stopping in the parking lot of a small strip mall where the most prominent business in the entire plaza appeared to be a bowling alley with an attached lounge. But then just as interestingly to the two detectives, the printing on the cheap plastic banner that hung above the front door of the bowling alley proudly confirmed that a country and western band was currently appearing in the lounge on Friday and Saturday evenings only.

So only as a precautionary measure, Peter and Don very wisely then decided to park their nondescript police car no nearer to the van than they thought would be prudent; even so, their location in the parking lot would still afford them the opportunity to be able to keep a close eye on the driver of the van.

Then as the situation continued to unfold, the two detectives found that they wouldn't have long to wait because just shortly thereafter a rather tall and somewhat thin young man with shoulder length hair exited the driver's side of the van. Thus after first retrieving a musical instrument case from the rear of the van, he then hurriedly began walking directly towards the entrance of the bowling alley and lounge.

Though at that point Peter and Don had already decided that it would be wiser for them to remain in their car for a few more minutes before they too would enter the bowling alley lounge.

Then once in the lobby Peter couldn't help but to notice that one of the posters in the window showed that their person of interest was not only a musician, but that he was clearly a member of a band called the "The Nashville Knights;" and which just happened to be the name of the group that was currently appearing in the lounge.

On the other hand, though, Peter and Don still didn't have any way of knowing for certain that the longhaired musician they'd been tailing was actually the man named

Frank; but then once inside the lounge they were able to ascertain the man's identity by simply asking one of the bartenders.

Then after returning to their vehicle, the detectives were even more curious about the longhaired musician's background; and particularly since Mrs. Burton had already confided in them the fact that Sandy had purportedly been involved in a relationship with a musician named Frank. Therefore, Peter and Don felt as if they already had enough probable cause to run the white van's license plate number through the Illinois Department of Motor Vehicles in order to obtain the longhaired man's true name and his proper home address.

From time to time, it seems as if homicide detectives are obliged to handle a multitude of task on a daily basis: it just simply goes along with standard police work. Then again, there are other times when it feels as though time is standing still as it must have seemed to Peter on that particular day since he still hadn't found the time to have the previous day's photos processed until that Saturday morning.

So mostly by connivance, but then also by burning a favor owed to him by a person in the police lab, Peter was able to put a rush order on the photos that they'd taken during the stakeout at Mrs. Burton's home. Then once the two detectives had the photos in their possession, they quickly headed back to the bar where Sandy was known to have last worked. Then fortunately for Peter and Don, the same two nuts that they'd previously interviewed just happened to be on duty when the detectives arrived at the Night Spot Tavern.

Of course Peter knew full well that the very next scene that was about to be played out in front of him was standard fare for the majority of all the noir types of detectives movies from the past and the present. "Have you seen this man?" Peter asked the bartender. Yet as he was doing so he knew that he must have sounded just like those old-time detectives in the movies who almost always asked the bartender that same old question.

Eventually, though, Peter was able to bring his thoughts back to the task at hand: and so he quickly then asked the two employees to take a close look at the photographs of Frank the longhaired musician. Then luckily for the detectives, both the bartender and the waitress were able to positively identify the man in the photo as being the same person who'd come into their bar on at least one prior occasion looking for work as a musician: and they also remembered that the man in the photo had stated that not only was Sandy a friend of his, but that, she would vouch for him.

By then, both Peter and Don sincerely believed that they had all of the circumstantial evidence that they would ever need in order to obtain an arrest warrant for their person of interest; therefore, they immediately called their lieutenant to advise him that they were bringing in a very solid suspect in the "Dumpster Case."

Of course along with all of the other relevant information that Peter and Don were interested in sharing with their lieutenant on that opportune day was the fact that they were also very interested in taking a good look at Frank the musician for the murder of the second young female homicide victim whose lifeless body had just recently been found in their district and who also had died as the direct result of a massive overdose of morphine.

All the same, it was already getting late on that very same Saturday evening before Peter and Don, who along with their lieutenant, were finally able to persuade an assistant D. A. to locate a judge that might be willing to sign the arrest warrant for their prime suspect.

Then regardless of the lateness of the hour, Peter and Don still weren't any too concerned about their chances of not being able to find their man since it was Saturday evening and which then meant that their person of interest would almost certainly be working in the bowling alley lounge that evening. Still, the two detectives wasted no time in returning to the bowling alley parking lot where they'd previously made plans to meet up with a small army of law enforcement officers which consisted of several members of the local village police department in addition to a couple of uniformed deputies from the Cook County Sheriff's Department.

When Peter and Don finally had their prime suspect tucked safely in an interrogation room back at the stationhouse, they discovered that their man of interest had indeed served in the U. S. Army during the Korean Conflict; and also that he'd been wounded in combat. That alone had made Peter wonder if perhaps the man's combat wounds might have had some bearing on the fact that the man named Frank had an obvious chemical dependency problem; then again, nothing in Peter's prior experiences as a law man could have ever explained why Frank had such an evil compulsion to murder innocent young women.

In the past, Peter had tried to live by an iron clad rule whereby he steadfastly refused to allow himself to become too emotionally involved in any one homicide case; but then after having worked the Sandy Burton homicide case he knew that he somehow felt differently. Therefore, Peter vowed that he wouldn't have any qualms in personally pulling the lever if the State of Illinois ever got around to strapping Mr. Frank Jefferies into the electric chair.

Then shortly there afterwards, all of the interested parties were assembled at Peter's stationhouse where the prime suspect in the "Dumpster Case" was officially arrested on one count of suspicion of murder; but then of course, they would all have to wait until the following Monday morning before their suspect could be formally charged in a court of law for the murder of Sandy Burton.

At that point in time the deputy prosecutors for the State of Illinois felt as though they'd already compiled enough circumstantial evidence against Frank Jefferies to at least go to trial with: but then once the authorities were allowed to search the suspect's apartment they not only found the knife which later would prove to be the weapon that'd been used to disfigure both of the young women in the morphine murders, but they'd also found several personal items in his apartment which had belonged to Sandy Burton and the other young woman whose lifeless body had been abandoned in a parked car.

Then too, all throughout the ensuing court procedures which followed the arrest of Frank Jeffries, both the representatives from the police department and the prosecuting attorney's office for the State of Illinois felt extremely confident that they had enough evidence to not only convict Jeffries of the two morphine murders, but that they'd also become very interested in the defendant for the murder of another young woman whose nude and morphine riddled body had just recently been found in an alley on the Westside of Chicago.

As Shakespeare once said, "Unnatural deeds do breed unnatural trouble."

DETECTIVE
CHICAGO POLICE
20588

Dead and Covered Up

Chapter One

Into the Line of Fire

Even as a child Paul Morris knew that he would one day have a career in law enforcement; and his greatest ambition in life was simply to follow in the footsteps of his father and grandfather who both had enjoyed illustrious careers while serving on the Chicago Police Department. Just the thought of being a policeman had always felt natural to Paul and especially since he'd heard nothing but the talk of police work, and of the solving of homicide cases, anytime that he was around his family.

Then once he was officially sworn in as a member of the force Paul would represent the third generation of the Morris family to have served on the Chicago Police Department. The old adage which says that "Apples don't fall far from the tree" is apparently true.

The far-reaching history of the Morris family's ability to produce excellent and dedicated homicide detectives began in the year of nineteen hundred and twenty-nine when Paul's grandfather, Detective Sergeant James Morris, served as the lead detective on the infamous St. Valentine's Day Massacre case. Thus as a direct result of his tireless investigative work on that one particular case,

James was able to retire as a Detective Lieutenant of the Homicide Division.

Then during the early nineteen fifties, Paul's father, homicide detective Peter Morris, was instrumental in the capture of a serial killer who'd terrorized the near North Side of Chicago for months on end; and by the end of his notable career Peter had attained the rank of Captain of the Chicago Police Department's Homicide Division.

And notwithstanding the fact that Paul had thoroughly enjoyed his first several years on the force while serving as a uniformed patrolman, he was a lot like the rest of the young patrolmen on the force which meant that he was constantly looking for excitement. However, Paul would soon learn that just the act of wearing a police officer's uniform could in and of itself prove to be both exciting and dangerous.

Then one evening, as Paul was performing his usual duties as a patrolman, he responded to a so-called leaky faucet type of radio call where he was supposed to make sure that the manager of a junior department store made it safely to his car after closing up his business for the evening.

In those days it wasn't all that unusual for a low priority call for assistance of that nature to be assigned to a one man car; and since Paul's regular partner, David Young, was still recuperating from a minor knife wound that he'd received during the previous evening's work, central dispatch had decided to use Paul's car number.

Consequently, then, when Paul arrived at the designated address at precisely 2100 hours, he proceeded to park his police cruiser near the intersection of Fortieth and West Madison streets. Then shortly thereafter, a man exited and then locked the side door of the junior department store. However, as Paul was approaching the man he assumed to be the store manager he couldn't help but to notice that the man had a bank deposit bag tucked under his arm. Moreover, when Paul asked the man if he'd informed dispatch that it was supposed to have been a bank drop call the manager readily admitted to his error but then said that his car was parked only a short distance away and that it was just on the inside of the alleyway which ran east from 40th Street.

So instead of calling it back it back in to dispatch like he knew he should have, Paul then very foolishly decided to walk the manager to his car just so he could hurry up and get the so-called routine call over with since it was nearing the time of evening when the night people started coming out. For as a rule, Paul preferred working the second or third watches since that's where the action usually is. In Paul's way of thinking, who in their right mind would ever want to work days with all of those normal and boring people out and about.

However, as Paul was walking alongside of the store manager, first on the sidewalk and then through the alleyway which ran due east towards Lake Michigan, he eventually realized that he'd either misunderstood the manager's instructions or else he'd been misled about how far away the car was actually parked. Ultimately, though, both Paul and the manager arrived near the spot where the manager's car was parked which was approximately one hundred and fifty feet due east from 40th street; and at that point in time the seemingly empty looking surroundings must have lulled Paul into a feeling of false security.

But when Paul finally reached the exact location where the manager's was parked he discovered that there were crossroads in the alleyway which not only ran both east and west, but that the alleyways also ran north-south.

Then to Paul's great surprise a car suddenly raced out of one of the hidden alleyways.

Thus by observing the erratic way in which the driver of the car was handling himself, it soon become apparent to Paul that the sight of a police officer's uniform must have rattled the nerves of the driver who then lost control of his car and which then caused him to crash into the rear of the manager's car.

At first glance, the driver of the runaway car appeared to have sustained only slight injuries from the crash; but the accomplice, who was apparently uninjured, then quickly jumped out of the damaged vehicle and began yelling that it was a stickup. After first grabbing hold of the back of the manager's suit coat, and then also by using the manager as a shield, the gunman began firing his pistol at Paul. Though luckily for Paul, the manager fainted straight away and which then gave Paul a clear line of fire. So as a direct result of Paul's quick actions two of the bullets from his pistol ended up striking the hold-up man squarely in the middle of his chest which felled him instantly to the pavement.

Remarkably, though, the driver of the holdup car was still somehow able to back his damaged vehicle away from the manager's car; but then instead of trying to escape he proceeded to drive directly towards Paul. And even though Paul managed to get off another two rounds from his service pistol, both of which struck the bandit in the face, the momentum of the out of control car caused it to continue on forwards until Paul was pinned helplessly between a brick wall and the manager's car. Although luckily for Paul, the manager soon regained consciousness and was able to use his cell phone to call in for assistance.

At first, Paul's injures were considered to be severe and even life threatening; and he felt that he was very fortunate indeed to have even lived through the terrible ordeal. But even after having survived a number of surgeries which were necessary to repair his broken and damaged body, Paul still had several months of intense physical therapy to look forward to before the doctors would release him to go back to work. However, Paul was still obligated to complete the psychological sessions which are always mandatory anytime that a police officer is involved in a shooting, and especially if the shooting results in a fatality.

DETECTIVE
CHICAGO POLICE
- CITY OF CHICAGO -
INCORPORATED 4th MARCH 1837
URBS IN HORTO

Chapter Two

Concentrate on the Woman

Ultimately, though, Paul was eventually released from the doctor's care; but then what followed next astonished almost everybody at the stationhouse, including Paul. Generally speaking, it's unusual for a police officer to advance as quickly in rank as Paul had managed to do: and even Paul was somewhat amazed by his own rapid promotion up through the ranks since he'd been wearing a police officer's uniform for only such a short period of time.

Paul had first learned of the change in duty from his Captain at the stationhouse: but then he eventually received an official letter from the main police headquarters informing him of his immediate transfer from the Radio Car Division to the Detective Division.

Change is, as they say, a constant and inevitable force and just three short years following the shootout in the alleyway Paul learned that the only partner he'd ever worked with in the detective division was planning a retirement party for the upcoming month of September. However, his partner's retirement wouldn't officially take effect until 1, January of the following year.

Paul's partner, Detective Sergeant Ken Walsh, had decided to do the twenty years and out for as everybody knows, twenty years of service on the Chicago Police Department, or any other police department for that matter, is usually enough for most. And even though Paul was sincerely happy for his partner's chance at living a normal life, the thing that bothered him the most was the fact that he and Ken were still deeply involved in a high profile homicide case.

It goes without saying that any homicide detective worth his or her salt would tell you that they would be willing to work just as hard to solve the murder of say a prostitute as they would if the victim happened to be an Alderman, or any other high public official. Yet having said that, Paul, along with everybody else on the force, knows full well that the solving of a low profile case will rarely if ever result in a promotion, whereas the solving of a high profile case might.

By thinking back to the first day that Paul had ever donned a police officer's uniform, and then especially right after his rapid promotion up through the ranks to the Homicide Division, it was somewhat understandable for Paul to hope and pray that he would have to solve just one high profile homicide case in order to earn the coveted Detective Sergeant's Gold Shield; and as luck would have it, the homicide case that he and Ken were currently working was just about as big as they come.

As a rule, promotions are extremely important to almost everybody on the police force; and therefore, the majority of all the major police departments in the United States, and then along with of course the U. S. Military, have a pay structure in place whereby they reward each rise in grade with an increase in pay by as much as ten percent. So when a person does the math they realize that the higher-up a person advances in rank, the more money they'll earn per year.

Therefore, Paul's personal dilemma was fairly simple in its nature: his partner would soon be retiring from the force and this then meant that Paul had only four short months left in which to work with the best detective on the entire Chicago Police Department; and it also meant that the two detectives had just four scant months left in order for them to solve an almost unsolvable crime.

The high-profile case in which Ken and Paul were currently working was the murder of a star Chicago Cub's baseball player who'd been shot and killed while standing at a window in his sixth floor, Lake Shore Drive condominium; and even though the entire ordeal was terribly difficult to make any sense out of, the two detectives had received a tremendous boost of support when they learned that forensics had determined that the bullet which had smashed into the head of the celebrated ballplayer could have only come from ground level.

At first, both Ken and Paul had thought it was incredulous that not one single person had seen or heard anything out of the ordinary on the evening that the ballplayer was murdered; for as customary, literally thousands of commuters had driven past that particular high-rise apartment building on that fateful evening. Furthermore, the twenty stories apartment complex was home to at least an additional hundred or so other condominium owners. Regrettably though, the canvass of all those other residents had not turned-up any viable eyewitnesses to the crime.

It goes without saying that Ken and Paul, and then along with, of course, all of the other members of the Chicago Police Department were well aware of the fact that they get paid to protect and to serve the citizens: so therefore, the police department as a whole had already accepted the fact that they would be the ones to feel the heat from the city fathers to solve this high profile case; but then to make matters even worse the local newspapers had been running almost nonstop daily stories since the month of June when the tragedy had occurred. Also just as understandably, the baseball loving community of Chicago had become so outraged by the senseless murder that they too had begun to demand immediate results from their police department.

However, all you can do is all you can do: and even law enforcement officers can only do so much before they too need a little rest and recuperation. Accordingly then, everybody in attendance seemed to thoroughly enjoy themselves when Ken held his retirement party at Kelly's bar.

Early on the following morning, however, when Ken and Paul arrived up at the stationhouse, albeit with a mouthful of cotton balls from imbibing a few too many cocktails, they were then summarily summoned into their Lieutenant's office. And on that particular morning their normally patient and tranquil boss, Lieutenant Harold Oxley, seemed to be more than a little anxious for a positive progress report on the case of the murdered ballplayer, which by then, had already become a real thorn in the sides of all the brass at the main police headquarters.

As a rule, Lieutenant Oxley was normally a well-grounded person but after having just received another round of early morning phone calls from the Mayor of Chicago, the Chief of Detectives, and several of the local newspaper journalists, it was somewhat understandable that the boss's even temperament had suddenly changed for the worse.

Who could blame the powers that be? Historically, the Chicago Cub's baseball team was seldom if ever the perennial favorite to win their division, let alone the World Series; but then during that spring season all of the local baseball pundits and swamis alike had proclaimed that the new year would be the year of the Cubs.

Then too, during that very same year, and also just as amazingly, something of great interest had taken place in the Chicago Cub's spring training camp. This strange and never before seen occurrence had come about when the new owners of the Chicago Cubs had decided to loosen their purse strings and which in turn had allowed the general manager to not only hire a team manager with a winning record, but he was also allowed to hire or trade for at least six all-star players.

Accordingly then, it was very unfortunate indeed when back in the month of June the Cubs had lost their National League batting champion; and this was especially disheartening to all the baseball fans since the Cubs had just taken over first place in their division. Then too, this senseless tragedy had to make some of the fans wonder if in addition to the "Curse of the Goat," there was to be another dreaded curse added to the already longsuffering history of the Chicago Cub's baseball team.

Consequently, then, it was at the conclusion of that early morning meeting with their Lieutenant that Ken decided to embark upon a new strategy in order to try to solve the case of the slain baseball player.

"Sign us out partner, we're going to do some old-fashioned police work," Ken said.

So after being directed by Ken, Paul then drove the two of them to an address on Milwaukee Avenue that was handedly located on the near North side of Chicago; and which then also just happened to be a part of a neighborhood that was most commonly known as Old Town. Then upon arrival, the two detectives entered an old building which had previously been home to a Y. M. C. A. but then according to the sign that hung above the entrance, the structure was now home to an association known as the N. C. T. H.

After first decoding this acronym for Paul, Ken told him that the letters on the banner stood for the North Chicago Transition Home and that it meant that the building was currently being used a shelter for the homeless.

Then once inside of the old building, Ken and Paul easily found the office which was located on the immediate right-hand side of the hallway. And as was customary for an older building of that type, the front of the office was adorned with an obligatory ¼ inch plate-glass window which included the obligatory round circle in the center of the window with which to speak through. Then after first stepping briskly up to the office window, Ken simply flashed his beautiful Detective Sergeant's Gold Shield.

By then, Paul had been a detective for a little over three years and during that time he thought he'd seen just about every type of reaction there was to see when a person first looked upon a police officer's badge. Nonetheless, when the pleasant looking, albeit slightly overweight young man standing behind the office window took note of Ken's badge he literally beamed at the two detectives as if they were his own long lost kinfolk. Then after studying the young man's face for only a moment or so, Ken spoke just one word; "Linus".

Hence by moving faster than his size should have allowed him to, the young man literally bounded out of the office door and then once in the hallway he thrust his out hand to Ken while at the same time introducing himself as David; this then was immediately followed by the statement that he was always glad to be of service to the law.

Thus with a goodly amount of enthusiasm, David proceeded to lead the two detectives down the old squeaky wooden-floored hallway until eventually they came to the end of the hall where he stopped before a door marked, "Conference Room." And with more than a modest show of deference, David bowed slightly before then hurriedly returning to his office.

Then somewhat surprisingly, the two detectives simply barged into the conference room without even knocking; and upon first glance, Paul couldn't help but notice that the man who was seated behind the desk appeared to be involved in a very intense conversation with the rather disheveled looking young man who was standing before him.

At first, the man behind the desk appeared to be more than a little startled by the detective's rude intrusion; but he quickly disregarded the interruption and then smiled that wonderfully disarming smile of his which God and Mother Nature had so blessed him with and then leaped completely out of his chair. Then notwithstanding the limitations of his somewhat slight stature, Linus proceeded to give his old friend Ken a big bear hug.

Next, Linus dismissed his charge from the room so that he and Ken could indulge in a few moments of exchanging pleasantries. Eventually, though, Linus remembered to invite the two detectives to follow him down the hallway where he said they could find some real coffee brewing in the employee's lounge.

Then once they were all seated in the lounge, Linus remarked that even though he'd kept in somewhat contact with his old friend Ken throughout the past several months and years, via the telephone, that it must have been awhile since he'd been around since he obviously had himself a brand-new partner. Linus also then stated that he'd already heard about Ken's late night retirement party at Kelly's bar.

"You still don't miss much, do you Linus?" Ken said.

"No sir detective Ken: but you do know that my cousin still swamps and cleans that bar," Linus said.

"Linus I want you to meet the famous gunfighter from the shootout at West Madison and Fortieth Street, detective Paul Morris," Ken said.

"Yeah, I seem to remember when that happened, it was about two years ago wasn't it?" Linus said.

"Actually, it was a little over three years ago," Ken, replied.

"So detective Ken what can I do you for today? Linus asked.

After first glancing over in Paul's direction, Ken spoke briefly to Linus about the slaying of the famous Chicago baseball player.

"I think it's time for us to take a look at this case from a different angle," Ken said.

"What do you ,mean?" Linus asked.

"Linus you might remember back in June of this year when some activists convinced the city council to hire the homeless and the disenfranchised in order to give them a chance to earn an honest living; and if I'm not mistaken, then some of your people were involved in that program. What I would like from you is a list of all the names of your people who participated in that experiment; and I would also like to have your personal take on each one of them. And Linus, there's one more thing, please make a note if any of the residents who were with you on that original work detail list are no longer staying with you," Ken said.

"No Problem detective Ken, I'll be right," Linus said.

Then upon his return Linus was asked to give the list to Paul who then studied it for a few minutes before eventually handing it over it to Ken.

"Detective Paul, did your partner ever tell you how he and I first met?" Linus said.

"Anyhow, that was way back when detective Ken was still in uniform and I was living on the streets where I was getting into one jam after another. Officer Ken used to kick my butt every time that he saw me on his beat until finally one day he decided that rehab might just do the trick; and then also just as thankfully, that's when he got me admitted into the Harbor House alcohol treatment center right here in Chicago. Then later on, after I'd been sober for a while, detective Ken recommended me for this here job; and for that, I will always be grateful," Linus said.

When Ken spoke again he was actually talking to Paul but he was looking directly at Linus.

"Linus has never been one of my personal informants; however, that's not to say that he hasn't helped me out in many other ways," Ken said.

"Paul when you're looking for someone who might have been involved in a crime then it's always helpful to have a friend who's been on the streets," Ken said.

"That's right Ken: but thanks to you I'm a completely different person," Linus said.

"Linus it might be farfetched to think that one of your residents could actually get his hands on an expensive high-powered rifle, let alone conceal it right here under your nose, but if you would be so kind as to conduct a thorough search of the building for me it would be greatly appreciated," Ken said

"And Linus, there's one more thing, when my retirement becomes official on the 1st of January I hope that you will still continue to help out my partner with any request that he may have from you in the future," Ken said.

"Please consider that as a personal favor from me to you," Linus said.

Then upon leaving the shelter, the two detectives returned to the stationhouse so that Paul could once again go through the old daily reports from the slain ballplayer's murder book in hopes of finding some small detail that might have been overlooked. Then while Paul was studying the murder book Ken was reiterating, and for at least the tenth time about where the shooter would have had to have been standing in order to have a clear view of the ballplayer's sixth story condominium window.

Though luckily for the two detectives, forensics had already determined that the fatal rifle shot could have only come from a small grassy lawn area which was located near the northeastern most portion of the apartment building: and therefore, the two detectives knew precisely where the shooter was standing when firing the fatal rifle shot; even if they still didn't have a clue as to the shooter's identity.

"Was the shooting simply a random act of violence or was it a premeditated act?" Ken said, as he mused aloud while continuing on with his dissertation.

"Paul since my job ends soon I'd like to share with you a tidbit of information about some of my more memorable experiences," Ken said.

"The secret to my modest success is very simple; always concentrate on the woman. Moreover, if you ever decide to use this time-tested rule of thumb piece of philosophy then it's always helpful if you can find a woman who's been scorned. It may very well be an old cliché but if used properly it can be a most valuable tool when it comes to solving crimes," Ken said.

Though as Paul continued on reading through the voluminous murder book he inevitably came across the notes that he and Ken had written about the slain ballplayer's widow.

"We never found any evidence of infidelity against the ballplayer's wife, nor did we ever find anything that even hinted that the husband was seeing other women," Paul said.

"That's true Paul: or at least we haven't found anything as of yet to suggest that either one of them was being unfaithful; but then again, perhaps we should re-visit the widow," Ken said."

"Sign us out partner," Ken said.

"By the way Paul, the Pittsburgh Pirates are scheduled to be in town this afternoon to play a doubleheader with our beloved Cubbies; and so later on why don't you and I make a run out to the friendly confines of Wrigley Field," Ken said.

Fortunately for the two detectives, the dead ballplayer's widow's condominium was located close by to Wrigley Field; and as expected, that same attractive woman with that same singsong South American accent answered the apartment door. Then once inside the apartment the detectives found that they were once again standing in front of the previously shot out insulated thermal window; and they also once more found themselves staring down at the small lawn area that was located some six stories directly below them from whence the shooter had supposedly fired the fatal shot.

All the same, after only a few more minutes of nothing but polite conversation with the widow, Ken and Paul thanked their host for her time and then headed for the first empty elevator that would deliver to the parking garage.

More importantly, though, all throughout their short drive over to the ballpark Ken and Paul were still counting their blessings for the re-appearance of a long lost report that'd been misplaced but had just recently been re-released by the Chicago Police Department's Forensics' Department.

According to the copy of the original report, it'd previously been determined that only the condominiums that were located on the northeastern most portion of the building had windows that faced both east and west as well as north; and therefore, the consensus was that only those specific apartment dwellers would have had any chance at all of witnessing the shooting.

Ken and Paul had both greatly appreciated the fact that they didn't have to re-canvass the entire hundred or so other condominium owners in the building; however, that still left some forty odd apartments where the occupants might have had a clear view of the small lawn area that was located directly below their windows. On the other hand, though, Ken and Paul had already canvassed those forty or so apartment owners and had done so on without any apparent success.

"How can that be?" Paul asked.

"Well Paul, if a person were to consider all of the other options that the condo owners had at their disposal on that particular evening, then it doesn't seem quite so farfetched to imagine that they might have failed to notice any unusual activity that was happening on the ground level below them. What with such a beautiful view of the park which sits to the north of the building, and then too, with Lake Michigan facing to the east, it's of no small wonder that we're having trouble finding anyone who could have witnessed the shooting. And on top of everything else that was going on that evening, the Chicago Cubs were finishing up the ninth inning of a televised baseball contest that just happened to coincide with the approximate time of the shooting," Ken said.

Then upon arrival at Wrigley Field, Ken somewhat belatedly informed Paul about the gist of an early morning phone call that he'd received from a Chicago land newspaper sportswriter that concerned an alleged fistfight which had purportedly taken place in the ballplayer's shower room at Wrigley Field.

"In addition to the significance of the fight itself, it seems to me that the most significant part of the story rest upon the fact that not only did the fight take place back in the month of June, but more importantly, the fight allegedly occurred just days before the unfortunate demise of the Cub's star baseball player," Ken said.

"I do seem to recall reading something about a fight in the clubhouse, but then later on the entire story ended up being squashed, Paul said."

"Get this Paul; the sportswriter who called me this morning also said that the identities of the two combatants in the shower room brawl were none other than the now deceased Cub's batting champion and an unnamed Cub's ballplayer. Furthermore, the sportswriter told me that he'd heard that the murdered Cub's batting champion was suspected of fooling around with another Cub's ballplayer's wife; or so the rumor goes. So to me, that helps to explain why our star baseball player was at home nursing his wounds on that particular evening instead of being out there on the baseball diamond with his fellow teammates," Ken added.

"To tell you the truth Ken, that's the first time that I've heard that rumor; then again, it really doesn't surprise me that much since we all know that boys will be boys," Paul said.

"There's another rumor that's also been running rampant amongst the ballplayers for quite some time now: and as you may already know, that one singular piece of gossip has been reported in at least one of the local newspapers. Amazingly, though, and as strange as it may seem, the essence of that particular story rest upon the fact that the Chicago Cubs had at one time seriously entertained the thought of trading their batting champion just so that they could alleviate some of the tension that was supposedly going on in the clubhouse," Ken said.

"Well Ken, batting champion or not, if the rumors were true then perhaps the Cubs should have let him go; for after all, he certainly wasn't in the same class as a Babe Ruth or even a Sammy Sosa," Paul said.

Then after arriving at Wrigley Field the two detectives decided to speak firstly with the Cub's trainer; for if there had been an altercation in the shower room back in June then the trainer would have had to tend to the injured participants. As a former Cub, the trainer was a legend in his own right; and besides being the present-day trainer he was also the team councilor. However, Ken thought that it was understandable when the Cub's trainer seemed to be somewhat reluctant to say much about the alleged fistfight between two of his better ballplayers. At the end of the day though, the trainer confided in Ken that the identity of the woman who the fight was supposedly over wasn't even the wife of a Cub's ballplayer after all but that she was actually the wife of a ballplayer who played for the Cub's greatest rival: the St. Louis Cardinals.

Also later on that same day, but only after they'd built enough nerve to do so, Ken and Paul were once again about to find themselves sitting in Lieutenant Oxley's office. Although on that particular occasion they were only there to ask their boss for a trip ticket to St. Louis, Missouri so that they could personally check out the rumor concerning the alleged affair between the murdered former Cub's ballplayer and the wife of a St. Louis Cardinal's ballplayer.

But then not so surprisingly, Lieutenant Oxley's face began turning red almost immediately after learning of this latest and most outrageous request coming from two of his most productive homicide detectives. For a while, the Lieutenant was so upset with Ken and Paul that he was unable to speak but then once he'd gained his composure he stated flatly that he was flabbergasted that the two detectives had the gall to show up in his office with a request of that nature; and especially since they'd already piled up a ton of overtime pay over the previous several months while investigating the ballplayer's death. Ultimately though, the Lieutenant finally gave in to Ken and Paul's request; however, he did so with some stipulations and conditions of his own.

"You two may drive a city car to St. Louis but you'll have to do it off the clock and on your own time," the Lieutenant said.

By the same token, Ken was feeling anything but discouraged on the way back to their desks; and even though it was completely out of character for him to do so he was literally beaming from ear to ear as if they'd just scored a huge victory.

"Paul my boy, this is a wonderful break for us: the Cubs are scheduled to be in St. Louis over the weekend in order to play the Cardinals a three game home stand," Ken said.

But since Paul wasn't what one might call a true aficionado of the game of baseball, he decided that while in St. Louis he would just as soon girl watch instead of trying to concentrate on the ballgame. However, Paul was even more pleasantly surprised when he learned that the baseball contest between the Cubs and the Cardinals was scheduled to be played on a Saturday afternoon; this then meant, of course, that the ballgame could possibly be over with by as early three-thirty or four o'clock P.M.; and therefore, his thinking was that if he did manage to get back to Chicago in time then perhaps he and his significant other might still have time to catch a late movie.

Thus at the conclusion of the baseball game, and then also just after the two detectives had finally found their car in the enormous Busch Stadium parking lot, Ken announced to Paul that he'd just received a cell phone tip from a sportswriter who worked for a newspaper in the St. Louis area. But then as Ken was explaining the gist of the call to his partner, he told Paul that the sportswriter who'd called him had categorically disavowed having any knowledge whatsoever about the rumor concerning the alleged affair between a Chicago Cub's baseball player and the wife of any of the St. Louis Cardinal's ballplayers; past or present.

To Ken, it was clear that the rumor which had portrayed one of the Cub's ballplayers as being a Romeo was indeed false and fictitious; and, that it was nothing more than just another loose and worthless dead-end. That is, of course, unless the sportswriter had disingenuously reported his findings; detectives are just naturally skeptical types of people, Ken thought.

Even so, all during the long drive home Paul began to realize that he was feeling a little put out by the fact that Ken was the one who was always getting those phone call tips and he wasn't. So when Paul finally got around to mentioning this minor resentment to his mentor he found that he was about to learn a valuable lesson.

"Paul my boy: a very wise man once said that if you help enough people get what they want, then they'll help you get what you want; or something similar," Ken said.

Then thankfully, the busy weekend was finally over and done with; and so naturally, the following Monday morning found the two detectives back working at their desks when Paul announced that the first thing he needed to do that day was to finish analyzing the names on the list that Linus had furnished them with.

As a matter of routine, Paul had, of course, already run the shelter's resident's names through the National Crime Information Center, or (N.C.I.C): in addition to the Chicago Police Department's Record's Division; regrettably though, he had not as of yet found anything of interest listed on their criminal yellow sheets.

"Well Ken, the majority of the residents at the homeless shelter have priors: however, their arrests and convictions consist mostly of the common garden-varieties of public intoxication and disorderly conduct; but then of course, there were also a few arrest listed on their records for indecent exposure such as urinating in public alleyways," Paul said.

"That seems to go with the territory," Ken said.

"But Ken there's more, out of all the residents who were on that original work detail list with Linus only three of them are no longer staying at the shelter. What's more, two of the missing men are not only still being held in the Cook County jail, but according to the court records those very same two men were in custody just prior to the day that the ballplayer was killed. Unfortunately though, the other missing resident seems to have completely fallen off the radar," Paul said.

"Well Paul, in all the years that I've been dealing with those types of people I've come to understand that it's not unusual for those kinds of transits to just up and disappear; then again, perhaps we should make another run over to the shelter," Ken said.

Sign us out partner", Ken said.

Even so, as they were en route to the shelter Ken confided in Paul that the main reason they were returning was to inquire about the one man that was still missing. Then upon arrival, the two detectives would once again end up drinking coffee in the employee's lounge with Linus.

During that particular visit, however, Paul was beginning to feel as though Linus wasn't being completely honest with them about the true status of the missing ex-resident. Furthermore, Paul felt as if Linus was intentionally being a little vague in his explanation about the missing man; that is, until Linus said that the man in question was okay except for an occasional lapse into alcoholism.

Then at the conclusion of their latest interview with Linus, and also being that it was almost noontime, the two detectives decided to take a lunch break before heading back to the stationhouse. Lunchtime was always the most dreaded time of the day for Paul and that was simply because of the fact that anytime Ken got near one of those Red-Hot, hotdog stands, for which Chicago was so famous, he would inevitably end up devouring at least one or two of the things. But then after returning to the stationhouse, Paul just happened to say something aloud that he was only thinking.

"Ken I'm getting some real bad vibes from Linus," Paul said.

"Why would you say something like that Paul, is it because Linus feels a certain loyalty to the street people?" Ken said.

"I'm not sure, it's just a feeling I have, that's all: and besides, you always say that we should concentrate on the woman; does Linus have one? Paul said.

"Sign us out partner", Ken said.

Approximately six blocks from the homeless shelter, and then cattycorner from an old Church, sat an average looking four-story Brownstone apartment building. Then after walking up just one flight of stairs, not counting the stoop, Ken stopped in front of apartment 2C.

In addition to the numeral and letter that were attached to the apartment door, there was also a small metal nameplate holder which held a typed piece of paper with the name of H. L. Meyers. And just moments later, the knock on the door was answered a woman who then cracked the apartment door open for an inch or two just so that she could peep out first before proceeding to remove the remaining several chains.

"I saw that it was you detective Ken: won't you come on in, the both of you," the woman said.

"Thank you Helen," Ken said.

"Helen I want you to meet detective Paul Morris," Ken added.

"My pleasure," purred Helen, with a mixture of Southern drawl and Western twang.

At first, Paul just nodded his head, but then he proceeded to halfway bow.

"Helen we just had a little talk with Linus so how's everything going with youse guys?" Ken said.

Then as if on cue, Helen began an almost endless tirade about having just recently caught Linus in a compromising situation with a woman who'd previously been employed at the shelter. Helen also then stated that her feelings were still smarting from the first time that she'd broken up with Linus which was back in the month of June after she'd learned that he was involved in a romantic tryst with an entirely different woman. But then in a more subdued voice Helen admitted to Ken and Paul that she and Linus had just recently tried to rekindle the old flame but that it hadn't worked out.

Surprisingly, though, Ken decided to end the conversation with Helen a little too abruptly for Paul's sake; and after thanking Helen for her time, Ken nodded his head towards Paul and the apartment door. Then once back in their car, Paul began to quiz Ken about his reluctance to ask Helen who'd given her that brand new shiner.

"There was no need to do that Paul because directly we're going to hear the truth from the guilty parties' mouth," Ken said.

Thus after driving the scant six blocks back over to the shelter, Paul wasn't any too surprised when Ken asked Linus to take a ride with them back to the stationhouse just so they could tie up any loose ends concerning the missing ex-resident. Then just shortly thereafter, the two detectives had Linus tucked safely away in an interrogation room where the three of them sat down for what would end up be a very interesting conversation.

Hence by reaching into his old bag of tricks, as Ken had done with thousands of other suspects in as many different cases, Ken appeared at first to be riffling through some important looking papers when he suddenly surprised Linus by telling him about the explanation that he Paul had just gotten from Helen concerning her views on the reason for their breakup. For a moment or two, Linus tried to play it off as if it were only as a big misunderstanding; but then after shrugging his shoulders somewhat nonchalantly, he said that it was a done deal with Helen.

"Linus, the Chicago Board of Public Works and Parks Department has just recently informed me that you personally chauffeured your crew over to that park on Lake Shore Drive on the very same day that the ballplayer was murdered: and if I'm not mistaken, that park is located right next door to the high-rise building where the deceased ballplayer formally lived; isn't that right,? Ken said.

"Yes sir, detective Ken, I believe that's true; but you see, I don't let my people stray too far from their work detail. And besides, we always carried our own sandwiches, drinks and such along with us when we went out on a cleanup job; and on that particular day, we even had our own handy rest rooms right there in the park," Linus said.

"Linus here of late I've had the opportunity to visit that particular park several times myself: and therefore, I happen to know that the northeastern most portion of that condominium building abuts the park; isn't that correct?" Ken said, and then by nodded his head towards the door he inferred that he wanted Paul to follow him out into the hallway.

"What do you think Paul? Ken asked.

"I think we should bring Helen in, post haste," Paul said.

Ken agreed, but then asked Paul to handle the situation by himself. Then while Ken was waiting in the hallway for Paul's return he just happened to stop in front of the interrogation room window where Linus was seated. Thus while standing there he was easily able to observe his old friend through the one-way mirrored glass. Yet as Ken was mulling the situation over in his mind, his twenty years of experience as a police officer was telling him that there was something about the picture that didn't quite fit; there seemed to be some pieces missing from the puzzle.

Nevertheless, when Paul returned to the police station with Helen in tow Ken asked him to stay in the interrogation room with Linus for a little while so that he could speak privately with her.

Though after a moment or two of mostly warm up conversation, Ken then very abruptly demanded to know from Helen just exactly who was responsible for the injury to her face. At first, Helen began to cry, but then once she'd gotten her emotions back in check she understandably became quite angry with Linus. Then by speaking in an almost whisper Helen told Ken that she was glad to have a friend like him because he was someone with whom she could vent her problems.

From the outset of their very long and detailed conversation it'd become obvious to Ken that Helen was no longer in love with Linus; and therefore, he encouraged her to tell him everything about her involvement with the man. Then luckily for Ken, Helen was more than happy to tell her story which began by reminiscing about the first time she'd ever met Linus which had been just shortly after her disabled husband had passed away.

"Just the thought of being a widow sorely depressed me, and so right then and there I decided that I would rather work for a living instead of going on the public dole; even though at that point in time I was legally entitled to receive the veteran's survivor's benefits. Accordingly, then, it wasn't long after my husband's funeral that I went to work at the men's shelter; and then shortly thereafter is when Linus moved in with me," Helen said.

"I remember when that happened," Ken said.

"Now Helen, about your deceased husband: if I'm not mistaken he was injured while serving in the United States Army; wasn't he?" Ken said.

"That's right detective Ken, he did receive some injuries while serving in the military: but even though he was somewhat disabled he was still able to participate in the Veteran's Memorial Burial Detail; and as a living testament to his personal courage he continued to fulfill that obligation up until the time of his death," Helen said.

"Well Helen since your deceased husband had served honorably in the military, and also being that he continued to be active with the burial team detail, I assume that he kept some firearms in the apartment," Ken said.

"Yes sir, detective Ken, he sure did: and at one point in time he kept both an Army Colt 45cal. automatic pistol and a M1 Garand Rifle which he used while on duty with the burial detail; but then of course both of those guns were always kept safely stored away in one of my closets," Helen said.

"So Helen, are the firearms still stored in your apartment?" Ken asked.

"Only the handgun is left detective Ken. For you see, Linus came to me one day and told me that he had to dispose of the rifle after it had malfunctioned while he was trying to fire it," Helen said.

"Helen I'm not intentionally trying to change the subject here but where did you go to work after you quit your job at the men's shelter?" Ken said.

"Well now let me see, detective Ken, I believe it was right after the time I'd quit my job at the shelter when a friend of mine told me about a temporary employment agency that was hiring; and so from then on, I just cleaned condominiums and such," Helen said.

"Oh Detective Ken: I think might have done something terrible back then. You see, I was working in that very same condominium building when that poor ballplayer got shot. Detective Ken you just don't know how I felt back in those days. At that point in time I was so out of my mind with jealously and anger after having just found out that Linus had betrayed me one more time that I felt like I needed to get some revenge; and so that's why I told Linus that I'd slept with that famous ballplayer while I was over there to clean his home." Helen said.

"Helen if you don't mind I'm going to need you to stay in this room for a little while longer; and then later on today we're going to need to take a statement from you," Ken said.

Thus by leaving Helen sitting alone in one of the other rooms, Ken was able to join Paul in the interrogation room where Linus was being interviewed. And then by nodding his head towards the door, Ken inferred to Paul that he wanted him to step out in the hall with him. Then once in the hallway, Ken told Paul to ask their Lieutenant for a warrant so that they could search the shelter. Ken also told Paul that in his opinion Linus was the shooter of the ballplayer.

At the end of the day, the police did find a rifle which had been carefully hidden away under a basement stairway; and as fate would have it, the gun turned out to be the murder weapon that was used to kill the famous ballplayer. In the end, however, it was nothing more than his personal guilt and remorse which had led Linus Mathis to confess to the crime of murdering the ballplayer. Accordingly, it was only matter of a few short months from the date of his confession that Linus was officially convicted in a court of law for the first degree murder of the former Chicago Cub's baseball player; and coincidently, the date of his conviction just happened to coincide with Ken's official retirement date.

As they say, time flies, and the month of January was soon upon them; and even though the situation between them was highly charged with emotion, Paul was intent upon helping Ken clean out his desk on the very last day on the job. However, Paul couldn't help but to show off his own brand new shinny Detective Sergeant's Gold Shield. Yet even as Paul was smiling warmly at Ken, he at the same time, couldn't help but to remind his mentor that he was right when he said that they should always concentrate on the woman.

DETECTIVE
CHICAGO POLICE
CITY OF CHICAGO
INCORPORATED 4th MARCH 1837

CHAPTER THREE

THE RABBI

As fate would have it, it turned out that Paul's new partner was a legend in the Homicide Division: however, his notoriety and fame had nothing to do with his ability to solve crimes for in that department he was woefully inadequate. The stationhouse gossip had it that the new man had worked out of practically every police station in the entire city: then again, what can you do with a police officer who's Rabbi just happens to be the Chief of Detectives; and on top of that, the Chief himself had thirty years plus on the job.

Then just as to be expected, the rumors concerning Paul's new partner continued to flourish all throughout the Homicide Division; and not surprisingly, the rumors about his new partner's Rabbi were becoming even more abundant. However, that's not to say that the Chief was without some clout of his own for it was a well-known fact that not only was he one of the highest-ranking officers in the Chicago Police Department who was closely connected to the Mayor's office, but that he was also known to be a friend of the Governor's. Also just as interestingly, some people said that the Chief of Detectives had friends in other high places such as Washington, DC.

All the same, Paul's new partner, detective Gary Materessi, did possess a few redeeming qualities of his own; and one of those attributes was that he knew more about the history of the Chicago Cub's baseball team than any other living person in the entire city of Chicago. More importantly, though, another wonderful quality which Gary possessed was that he loved to canvass crime scenes; and that asset alone had just naturally endured him to all the different partners he'd worked with throughout the years he'd been on the force.

At an earlier time, however, and this was back when Ken and Paul were in the midst of working a cold case, Paul had inadvertently come across an old daily report that Gary had written for a homicide case that he'd worked in the far distant past; and the sum total substance of the language that Gary had used in the report had given Paul an insight into the workings of his new partner's mind.

There was another rumor that'd been going around for years which said that Gary Materessi had always considered himself to be a yet undiscovered and a much underappreciated writer. Consequently, that one self-flattering bit of egotism had more than likely caused him to repeatedly embellish his daily reports with such flowery sentences as, "She was spherically wrapped in a perfumed aura which consisted of a yellow and white polka dot dress." In that one particular instance, Gary had apparently used those overly descriptive words to describe the clothing worn by a female homicide victim; is that what they call a double intend ere`? Paul wondered. So for Paul, it was a simple matter for him to deduce that those types of discrepancies, and possibly many more, were among the primary reasons for the majority of Gary's transfers. Even so, anytime that a police officer has a Rabbi who wields as much power and influence as the Chief of Detectives there's really not much left for Gary's superiors to do but to transfer him to a different district.

Then too, it was also widely known throughout the squad that Gary held the rule of seniority in very low disdain: then again, everybody on the force knows full well that anytime that a detective has more time on the job than their partner, then more often than not that person would just automatically become the senior member of the team. Though as time would tell, the legitimacy of that age-old custom was about to be challenged when detective Gary Materessi arrived at Paul's stationhouse. Hence, once Gary was officially a member of Paul's squad, he then very quickly announced that even though he had twenty years of experience on the job, he had no desire whatsoever to become the lead or senior detective on any team. And yet, detective Gary Materessi's arguments on that particular point would soon become stilted and needless when he learned that his new partner, Paul Morris, had just recently been promoted to the rank of Detective Sergeant.

Then luckily for Paul and Gary's sake, the first two homicide cases that they caught as a team were slam-dunks from the very beginning. In the Homicide Division, there's one irrefutable fact that nearly all of the experienced detectives can agree upon and that's simply that when friends and family members attempt to practice the art of murder, then those cases tend to be some of the easiest ones to solve. And that would ring especially true if the suspects are prone to feelings of guilt and remorse, of which they so righteously deserve, and which then would also cause them to be much more eager to confess to their terrible crimes; then again, it also helps if the suspects have been introduced to the ploys of a well-disciplined team of homicide detectives.

As a rule, amateur killers tend to ignore one of the most important ingredients in the total equation when they first attempt to get away with their hideous deeds; and that's simply the fact that they don't usually take into account the tremendous amount of experience that the average homicide detective can bring to the table.

Generally speaking, the majority of police officers are well aware of the fact that most homicides are committed by first time offenders; and therefore, the guilty parties have only one shot at trying to make their ridiculous lies believable. On the other hand, though, some of the more seasoned homicide detectives might have already investigated even well over a hundred cases of murder.

There are times, though, when it seems as if crime never takes a holiday; but then during one particular morning, while Paul was working at his desk after what'd been a most hectic several months of investigating a multitude of fresh homicide cases, he was more than a little grateful that they were experiencing one of those uncharacteristically slow periods at the stationhouse where he was fortunate enough to find the time to read the morning newspapers. And in bold print, the headlines on that morning's newspaper would confirm that the rumors which had been floating around the department for several months were apparently all true.

The gist of the front-page story was that the State of Illinois had just recently built more new prisons than all of the neighboring states combined. Conversely, though, the composer of that startling essay on prison reform was more than willing to give the credit for the building of the additional prisons to the newly elected members of the Illinois General Assembly at the State Capital in Springfield who'd previously threatened to get tough on crime; and this time they'd finally decided to do it.

Something strange and unusual was happening alright, Paul thought, for here of late, many of the white-collar felons, and even a few of the perpetrators of crimes of passion, had been set free on early release. However, the career criminals, the hard-core junkies, and then along with, of course, all of the other people who lived by the gun had suddenly found themselves locked up behind bars; and, the proverbial key had been thrown away for good.

But then also just as amazingly, it appeared to Paul that this new and strange phenomenon had done what many a naysayer had said would be impossible; and that's simply that the hardened and violent criminals wouldn't get a chance to repeat their crimes against humanity because the State of Illinois had decided to keep them imprisoned.

Oh sure: the murder rate behind the razor-sharp concertina wired walls of the numerous Illinois prisons had begun to increase dramatically. Yet when the newspaper journalists finally got around to polling the average person on the street, then the citizens would just smile and say; "Well it's better for them to kill each other off than it is for us to have to die."

All the same, the drastic changes within the prison system itself would eventually force the hierarchy at the Chicago Police Department to try to find some new and improved methods on how best to conduct their day to day business; and consequently, the changes in procedure would also force the police brass to come up with better ways in which to use the resources of law enforcement which had suddenly become so much more readily available to them.

The new polices at the Illinois Department of Corrections were certainly having a tremendous effect upon all of the different jobs within the numerous divisions of the Chicago Police Department but no division was feeling the effects of the changes quite like the Homicide Division where dozens of detectives had suddenly found themselves working cold cases.

The rehashing of cold cases has always been standard procedure within most of the major police departments throughout the country; however, it's usually only done when the business of crime is extremely slow and the murder rate is way down.

Remarkably, though, Paul's boss had his own distinctive and novel way of handing out cold cases. Lieutenant Harold Oxley's own personal method of distributing the cold cases was to assign a case to the senior detective of a team by matching the first initial of the lead detective's last name with the first initial of the victim's last name. For instance, if the senior detective's name happened to be Brown, then that detective would catch a cold case with a name of a victim that began with a B. Therefore, since Paul's last name was Morris, with an M., then Paul and his partner caught a cold case by the name of McGregor.

Though while working cold cases it was only natural for Paul to remember the good old days when he and Ken had worked together; and every now and then he still found himself secretly wishing that he and his old partner were back together. Although if Paul were to be completely honest with himself then he would have to admit that even when he and Ken had worked cold cases then they too had found them to be extremely difficult to solve; then again, that was primarily due to the fact that so many of the witnesses had either expired, or else they'd simply moved away from the area.

Even so, there was at least one good consolation which had come out of the new system of having to temporarily work mostly cold cases; and that simply was the fact that the close ratio wouldn't count against their average percentage of solving homicide cases.

And since Paul and Gary were trying to get a running start with their new cold case, they decided to take the old McGregor murder book into the evidence room with them for what would end up being a most boring two hours while they sifted through the victim's personal belongs.

By the same token, Paul was luckily enough to find a few items which had been stored away in the old McGregor box of evidence that seemed to be a little more interesting than the others; and one of those was the murder weapon itself which just happened to be an old 38-caliber revolver. Generally speaking, however, the guns that are used in homicide cases aren't necessarily that dissimilar from one another; that is, of course, with the exception of the differences in the caliber.

On the other hand, though, Paul felt that the handgun which had been used in the old McGregor slaying was by far the most interesting item in the entire evidence package; but then of course, that was primarily because of the fact that someone had apparently used acid on the handgun in order to carefully remove the serial number from the old pistol. And because of his experiences in law enforcement, Paul knew that that feat alone would have required of a person to have a certain amount of technical knowledge and skill of just exactly how the science of forensic evidence works. Paul was also well aware that the majority of the veteran police officers on the street almost always refer to a handgun of that type as either a throw away piece or a drop weapon.

In due course, their work in the evidence room was eventually completed; but as they were headed back towards their desks Gary chirped what's next boss? Just the idea of having Gary call him boss irritated him somewhat. Still, Paul decided not to mention it at the time because something of great interest had caught his attention while looking through the old McGregor murder book.

"Sign us out Gary, we're taking a ride to a hospital," Paul said.

The hospital Paul had in mind to visit was conveniently located on the Southside of town and just happened to be fairly near to the intersection of 29th and California Streets. In Paul's way of thinking the location of the hospital was particularly relevant to the cold case since the hospital was situated across the street from the California Street Park where the murder of the young McGregor lad had taken place. For as Paul had previously noted while reading through the old murder book, one of the first incident and complaint reports ever written on the McGregor homicide case stated that a certain female employee of the hospital just happened to be the first person to notice the young homicide victim lying on the ground.

First and foremost, though, Paul realized that it was somewhat doubtful that the woman would still be working at that same hospital some twenty years later; he did, however feel that it was still worth a try. A phone call to the hospital would have certainly been more prudent but to Paul's way thinking it was a nice day outside and so what the heck.

Upon arrival at the hospital then the first thing that the two detectives had planned on doing was to stop by at the information desk; and from there, they were, of course, directed to the personnel office where they would learn if they had any chance at all of obtaining such pertinent and private information regarding a past or even a present employee.

Even so, both Paul and Gary were pleasantly surprised when they discovered that not only was Nurse Marie Gonzales still working at the hospital, but that she was presently working the three to eleven o'clock P. M. shift. So after first cajoling the nurse's address from the personnel clerk, they then headed directly for the neat little town house where the nurse lived, which as it happened, was located on the Southside of town and was handedly situated nearby to the intersection of Thirty-Fifth and Halstead streets.

As a rule, Paul believed in his heart of hearts that if you were ever fortunate enough to find a witness with some medical training then you are way ahead of the game; and especially since most medical people are trained to be more aware of their surroundings; then too, they're always more observant of other people's injuries.

Still, the working of cold cases was once again about to show Paul just exactly how much more difficult they are to work; or at least, when they're compared to fresh homicide cases. And even though Nurse Gonzales seemed to be blessed with a good memory, she'd also made it a point to let the two detectives know that this was at least the third time in the past several years that the police had stopped by with questions for her. Then as if to prove her point to Paul and Gary, the nurse stated that the other detectives had asked her all of the same old questions; so naturally, Paul felt as if Nurse Gonzales had almost certainly given all of the other detectives the same old answers. So with their conversation going nowhere Paul thanked the nurse for her time then and left her one of his personal police business cards as the two detectives politely excused themselves from the situation.

By then, it was almost noontime and so Paul suggested to Gary that it seemed like a good time for them to take a lunch break. Then while eating their lunch, Paul was reflecting on the differences between the past and present lunchtime options. At least nowadays he was somewhat thankful that he no longer had to eat Red-Hots every other day. But instead of having to eat nothing but hotdogs for lunch he now had to listen to Gary's incessant reiteration about the entire history of the Chicago Cubs. As was fast becoming a common and usual lunchtime tradition, Gary posed a question to Paul and the lesson on that particular day centered upon the history of Wrigley Field.

"Paul, did you know that Wrigley Field was originally built for the sole use of the Federal Baseball League? But that the ballpark stayed in their hands for only about three years before eventually being taken over by the National Baseball League?" Gary said.

And even though Paul was somewhat of a Cub's fan himself, he at the same time was a lot more interested in trying to stay focused on the McGregor case; so therefore, he immediately directed Gary's attention back to the interview that they'd just conducted with the nurse.

"What good is a witness to a twenty-year old homicide case who still sees the same old thing in her mind every time that she thinks about it?" Paul said.

"None whatsoever: and that's why cold cases are so tough to crack," Gary said.

Thus following their lunch break, the detectives then hurriedly returned to the stationhouse just so Paul could once again study the old McGregor murder book. Yet as Paul was reading through the old daily reports on the McGregor case he just happened to come across an old summary report that caught his eye. To Paul, it was abundantly clear that the detective who'd written those old reports had meticulously listed all the names of the rubbernecking onlookers who were standing anywhere nearby to the vicinity of the crime scene; but to Paul's big surprise, Gary's name was included therein.

Still, when Paul queried Gary as to why his name had appeared in the old summary report he got the explanation from his partner that at that point in time he was working his way through college; and also that he just happened to be on duty at the hospital on the very same evening when the McGregor lad was murdered. Gary then stated further that it was just right after he'd first come outside when he noticed that both the Medical Examiner and the police Crime Scene Investigators were still working the crime scene; and coincidently, that was also when some gray-haired detective approached him and asked for his name.

"To tell you the truth Paul, the events of that evening had a tremendous effect on me. I was so impressed with the efficiency of the professionals that I witnessed doing their jobs that evening that I decided right then and there to change my college major over to the study of Criminal Law; and also that same evening I decided that I would eventually end up having a career in law enforcement," Gary said.

DETECTIVE
CHICAGO POLICE
CITY OF CHICAGO
INCORPORATED 4th MARCH 1837

Chapter Four

The Art of Working Cold Cases

The lead detective on that twenty some odd year-old California Street Park homicide case just happened to be a grizzled old man by the name of Shawn O'Riley; but Paul's immediate concern was that O'Riley had retired from the force some eight years after having worked the McGregor case. On the bright side, however, O'Riley had continued to live in the Chicago area; and so when Paul contacted the Chicago office of the Fraternal Order of Police on Washington Blvd. he learned that O'Riley had just recently moved in with his daughter who luckily lived nearby in one of the suburbs.

Therefore, the next logical stop on Paul and Gary's list of things to do that day was to drive out to the daughter's home which was conveniently located in the village of Oak Park, Illinois.

So when O'Riley learned of the true nature of their visit he was more than happy to rehash old times with them. Regrettably though, when Paul looked upon the gaunt and drawn face of the old detective he could not only could see the ravages of time imprinted there, but he could also see the effects of a major medical condition that O'Riley would have eventually to deal with.

Conversely, after first recalling some of the more important facts of the McGregor homicide case for Paul and Gary, O'Riley stated that instead of looking for answers on the outside of the hospital, he and his partner had decided to focus their time and energy on taking a good look at the employees. Ultimately, though, O'Riley had to admit that nothing much had ever come out of their investigation. He did, however, admit that was primarily due to the fact that they'd failed to uncover any hard evidence against any one particular suspect. So then after first thanking their host for his time, the two detectives took their leave.

"So Gary: what's your read on O'Riley? I mean, what do you think of his theory?" Paul said.

"Could be: because you see when I worked at the hospital there were several incidents where a few of the employees were caught red-handed while breaking into the drug cabinets: and from then on, and then all throughout the ensuing crackdown which ensued at the hospital, there were several situations in which some of the people actually ended up getting fired for theft; and a few of them were sent packing right in the middle of their shifts," Gary said.

"Well Gary, at first it appeared to me that the young man's murder might have been a random act of violence but that was before I came across a very interesting piece of information while reading one of O'Riley's old notes", Paul said.

In short, Paul shared the contents of one of O'Riley's notes with Gary in which the old detective had written that the nineteen-year-old male victim was supposedly a homosexual. And since the evening was still young Paul made the proposition that it might be wise for them to see if they could locate the parents of the victim. Although at that point in their conversation Gary stated that he had some personal business which desperately required his immediate attention; and therefore, he would just as soon beg off for the rest of the evening. Of course Paul replied that it was fine with him and he told Gary that he would see him on the following morning at the stationhouse.

Yet later on that same evening, as Paul was sitting alone in the squad room, he couldn't help but to think about Gary's personal life; or the lack of it thereof. Paul didn't necessarily believe that he was the only one in the squad who felt that Gary was a little different from all the rest of the detectives; and especially since it was fairly obvious to everybody else at the stationhouse that Gary was such a loner. Moreover, nobody in the squad had ever seen Gary in public: or for that matter, no one had ever seen him in a cop bar; except perhaps, on those few rare occasions when he'd felt obligated to attend a fellow officer's retirement party.

DETECTIVE
CHICAGO POLICE
- CITY OF CHICAGO -
INCORPORATED 4th MARCH 1837

Chapter Five

The Mentor

In the past, there'd been times when just the act of driving full out on one of the local highways had helped to clear Paul's head somewhat; and so after leaving the stationhouse where he'd been thinking mostly about Gary, he ended up driving his rather too powerful personal car a little too fast on one of the local expressways.

Paul was a thirty-five year old Detective Sergeant Policeman who definitely should know better than to speed; then again. somewhere in the back of his mind lurked a silly notion that if the Highway Patrol Division did happen to pull him over then perhaps his having a badge would help to get him out of a ticket. It'd happened to him once before and he'd been fortunate indeed to have gotten off with only a stern warning from an officer who'd told him that he really should know better since that he was a police officer himself.

Eventually, though, Paul was able to exit the expressway safely; but then instead of going on home like he'd intended, he ended up stopping by at a neat little Pizza Bar on the Westside of town where he proceeded to engage in a couple of hours of cop talk with a few of the other off duty police officers. However, boredom soon set in and after drinking only a couple of beers Paul decided to call his ex-partner, Ken Walsh.

Paul didn't really wish to intrude upon his ex-partner's private time, but on that particular evening he felt that he needed to talk to his old mentor. So when Ken invited him to do so, he just naturally agreed to drive on up to his old friend's home.

It's strange, thought Paul, he had a brother and a sister plus two wonderful parents: and which one of which was even a retired police officer; but at that point in time the only other person in the whole world he really cared to talk to was his ex-partner. In his heart of hearts Paul considered Ken to be the best detective in the entire city of Chicago; whether he was still on the job or retired.

When Ken retired from the force, he and his wife had decided to move to the community of Evanston, Illinois just so they could live close to their daughter who was a graduate of Northwestern University. Then luckily for Paul, the long drive up north seemed to help clear his head somewhat and then soon after arriving at his old friend's home he was told that Ken's wife, Betty, was at their daughter's house baking grandmother cookies. So with Ken leading the way, the two detectives made their way back towards the kitchen area where Ken thoughtfully remembered to ask Paul it was okay before handing him one of the two beers that he'd just pulled out of the fridge.

"Sure Ken, it's all right, and besides, I've only had two other beers this evening and that was about an hour or so ago. You know, it's just like the instructors at the Police Academy told us: the human body can metabolize about one ounce of alcohol per hour, and which then means that a one hundred and seventy-five pound man can safely drink about six beers in a three hour period, or something like that; anyhow, who bothers to even count after having drunk that many beers, right Ken?" Paul said, as both men laughed.

"Well Paul, why don't you have a seat and then tell me all about your new partner? Ken said.

At first, Paul only jokingly rolled his eyes up into his head, but then he had to laugh aloud as he remembered some of his partner's personal quirks and idiosyncrasies.

"Gary's a great crime scene canvasser," Paul said.

"So I've heard," Ken said.

"To tell you the truth Ken, he's kind of hard to work with, you know; and expressly since he has all of that clout downtown. To be honest with you Ken I even sometimes wonder if he keeps a tape recorder hidden away somewhere in his pockets," Paul said.

"Well Paul, he wouldn't be the first cop to do that; now would he? What was that cop's name in New York City, was it Serpico?" Ken said.

"And Ken, there's something else that's strange about him: do you happen to remember an old case from several years back when a nineteen year old boy was found shot dead in the California Street Park?" Paul said.

"I do seem to remember something about that particular case: it was about twenty some-odd years ago and if I'm not mistaken then O'Riley caught that case," Ken said.

"Yeah, well, we talked to O'Riley today and he's not doing too well," Paul said.

"Sorry to hear that Paul: O'Riley was an excellent cop who was well-known throughout the department to be honest and thorough to a fault," Ken said.

"I heard that you guys were working cold cases," Ken said.

"We sure are: and just today we stopped by at this nurse's home who was supposedly one of the few witnesses to the California Street Park, McGregor murder;

or at least, she was one of the first persons to arrive on the scene," Paul said.

"But Ken, that's not the real clincher here: but rather, it was later on in the day after we'd returned to the stationhouse after interviewing the nurse when I noticed that Gary's name was listed in one of O'Riley's old notes," Paul said.

"And get this Ken, Gary didn't even bother to tell me that he was working at the hospital on the very same evening that the young man was killed; and in addition to that, he also failed to mention the fact that he'd been interviewed by O'Riley," Paul said.

"And so what's your point, Paul?" Ken said.

"Nothing and everything: but don't you think that something of that nature would be the type of thing that you would just naturally want to share with your partner?" Paul said.

"And as you may already know, this guy Gary is such a mysterious loner and all," Paul said.

"Well Paul, perhaps you should give Gary a little more time and then if it still doesn't work out you could always ask your Lieutenant to get you another partner," Ken said.

"But Ken, I've never done anything like that before, it would feel strange," Paul said.

"Well Paul, with Gary's track record from the past I really don't think that anyone could fault you if you were to ask for a new partner. Then again, perhaps you shouldn't be in such a rush to judgment here because there might be a logical explanation for everything that's happened so far; and Paul, there's something else to consider here, there's always the possibility that Gary might have just simply forgotten about being at the hospital that evening," Ken said.

Then after meditating on that statement for moment or so, Paul said that Gary was much easier to work with when they had fresh homicide cases to work because then, all he had to do was to ask him to canvass half of the city of Chicago; and then of course, that would also keep him out of his way for a while. Both men laughed.

"Thanks for the beer, Ken," Paul said.

"Anytime friend, and you're welcome to come back again, real soon," Ken said.

On the long drive home Paul once again found himself wishing for a partner like his old friend Ken; still, Paul knew that was simply because Ken was someone with whom he could discuss almost anything that was bothering him.

Nevertheless, the following day was a workday and so the very first thing that Paul took care of after arriving at the stationhouse that next morning was to check the case board on the squad room wall where he noticed that there were two teams of detectives ahead of him and Gary on the next two fresh cases of homicides that were almost certainly bound to come in; and so Paul asked Gary to sign them out for the morning.

Then upon arriving at the police parking garage Paul asked Gary to do the driving over to the residence of the parents of the deceased McGregor youth so that he could have a chance to re-read the old notes from O'Riley's daily reports. Then shortly thereafter, the two detectives were just preparing to knock on the front door of the McGregor residence when they were suddenly confronted by a neighbor man who demanded to know who they were looking for.

Then after identifying himself and Gary as police officers, Paul explained to the neighbor man that they were re-investigating the homicide of the young

McGregor lad. Then not only did the neighbor man identify himself as being the eldest of the McGregor boys, but he said that he was also a brother to the deceased McGregor boy.

Michael was also quick to point out that he and his family members had spoken with several other detectives throughout the past twenty years and that they still didn't have any new or pertinent information regarding the slaying.

Paul quickly apologized to Michael for the intrusion but then told the brother of the murdered McGregor boy that he might still be of some help to them if only he could help them clear up one point of interest; and even though Michael was somewhat reluctant to do so, he eventually agreed to cooperate with the two detectives. Paul's question to the neighbor man was simple and to the point: he asked Michael if he'd ever wondered whether his brother's lifestyle and sexual preference had played any role in this terrible tragedy.

To some extinct, Michael seemed a bit unwilling to answer Paul's question on such a sensitive subject; however, he finally did admit to Paul that he hadn't known just quite what to think about his brother's death; that is, until he finally came to his own conclusion that in all probability his brother's lifestyle had nothing at all to do with his death. Then next, however, Michael abruptly changed the subject by asking Gary if he'd grownup in Mayor Daley's old neighborhood.

"Yes sir I did: as a matter of fact I grew up in the area of 47th and Halstead," Gary said.

"You're a little older than I am but I thought you looked familiar," Michael said.

Nonetheless, when Michael McGregor spoke again he might have unknowingly revealed some of his own heartfelt and sincere emotions by saying that he wished his family had never moved over into the California Street Park area; and then added, that if they hadn't, then this whole tragic affair might never have happened.

Then after returning to their car, Paul told Gary that he had him figured for a suburbs type of a guy.

"No sir, Paul: I grew up in the father of Chicago's old neighborhood; and by that I mean, of course, is that my family once lived nearby to the home of the former mayor of Chicago, the honorable Richard J. Daley himself. As a matter of fact, a great number of my relatives were members of the Mayor's Volunteer Citizen's Reserve Police Force which at one point included a group of ten thousand strong special deputies," Gary said.

"It was kind of a neighborhood watch sort of thing," Gary said, and then smiled.

"Anyway, the whole bunch of us used to hang around that old pink castle style of a home where the Mayor once lived; and if memory serves, the mayor's old home even had a few of those round turrets on the top. Yes sir Paul, we grabbed hold of the Mayor's coat tails and road them all the way to city hall; and then of course, some of the old neighborhood gang, like the Chief of Detectives before me, and then eventually myself, went on to become members of the Chicago Police Department," Gary said.

Then the next stop on their agenda on that busy day was at the stationhouse where Paul planned on asking Gary to search through all the available police records for the past twenty years that had anything at all to do with the McGregor case; and then to also pull up everything interesting that he could find listed on the Tribune Web Pages. In the meantime, Paul personally pulled up of the

McGregor files that were still available in the crowded record's room.

Also later on that same day, Paul phoned the security office at the hospital in hopes of obtaining some additional information on the drug thefts which had occurred at approximately the same time of the McGregor slaying; unfortunately, though, all of that day's hard work and research had turned out to be just another dead-end. Meanwhile, though, Gary was keeping himself busy by making copies of all the files that he could find on the McGregor cold case.

Even so, something new and unexpected was about to rear its ugly head and that was the old adage of "Murphy's Law" which states that if anything can go wrong then it probably will. Therefore, try as we might, some days just don't come out as well as we'd planned them so after poring over the same old documents for another several hours it was thankfully time for the two detectives to call it a day.

On that particular evening, however, Paul was more than a little pleased to be getting off work at a fairly decent hour since he had plans to attend a class at Northwestern University where he was studying the comparatively new science of human genetics and D. N. A.

It was also at about that same point in time when Paul began to realize that it was beginning to be a struggle to just keep up with all the latest F. B. I. reports concerning a notable and substantial increase in the numbers of homicides that were occurring on the nation's roadways.

Thus according to another report which had just recently been released by the Feds, it was noted that most of the law enforcement agencies across America had noticed a definite spike in the number of serial killers which appeared to be operating at free will across the nation which had begun to increase incrementally at about the same time that the interstate highway-system was introduced to the nation.

Also during that same period of time, and not just by a matter of chance, the F. B. I. had become seriously interested in the study of the so-called modern-day phenomenon of serial killers. Accordingly then, it was inevitable that the F. B. I. would become the first law enforcement agency in the U. S. to develop a new investigating division in hopes that they could learn how to profile this new breed of criminal which was rapidly becoming a real menace to the nation.

Then too, the people at the F. B. I. who were in charge of keeping those kinds of statistics, had noticed early on that the total numbers of serial killers had not only increased dramatically but that they'd become more evenly spread out across the country. The Feds had also learned that the majority of those serial killings had occurred in and around the major U. S. cities which were closely connected to the interstate highway system.

Therefore, it was certainly no surprise to the people in law enforcement when the F. B. I. decided to initiate a nationwide training program so that the local members of the various law enforcement agencies around the country could receive their profiler's training classes directly from their regional universities instead of having to travel all the way to the main F. B. I. headquarters in Washington, DC.

Accordingly then, when the Chicago Police Department, along with all of the other major police departments across the country began to see the need for such training then they too elected to enroll a few of their more proficient homicide detectives into the profiler's classes. And luckily for Paul, he was fortunate enough to be included in one of the training classes; but Paul knew that it would also look good in his personnel file.

CHAPTER SIX

HOMICIDE: UNFORTUNATE BUT ROUTINE

On the following morning, just as Paul was entering the squad room he was straight away corralled by his Lieutenant who handed him a fresh homicide case. According to the paperwork this new senseless tragedy had apparently begun over a simple fender-bender type of automobile accident but had evolved into a case of road rage before then ultimately escalating into a shooting with a fatality. Then notwithstanding Paul and Gary's intense desire to hurriedly study the paperwork on their new road rage/homicide case, they at the same time were still trying to have a conversation with the daytime Desk Sergeant. The sergeant in question had not been on duty at 2200 hours on the evening past: however, as everybody in the stationhouse can attest to, Desk Sergeants are almost always more knowledgeable about the daily operations of a police station than the Lieutenants or the Captains are.

But since Paul and Gary weren't the designated lead detectives on the road rage case, they therefore didn't have the primary responsibility to solve their district's latest homicide; even so, they'd noticed that the night watch detectives had done a fairly decent job of investigating the new case.

In that particular case of road rage/homicide, the police were very fortunate to have come up with three separate eyewitnesses who'd all agreed upon the make and model of the shooter's vehicle; but then to everybody's big surprise, one of the eyewitnesses had even furnished them with a license tag number.

So notwithstanding the fact that the night watch detectives had been unable to find anybody at home at their road rage suspect's last known address, they'd nonetheless done the next right thing by requesting that all of the officers working out of the district's motor patrol and radio car divisions should continue to cruise by their primary suspect's residence during the previous evening in hopes of locating their person of interest. But then later on that morning, and much to everybody's surprise, the officers in the squad were in for a big surprise when both the road rage suspect and his attorney came strolling into the stationhouse; this then meant, of course, that the lead detectives had to hurriedly return to the station just so they could read the suspect his Miranda rights.

First and foremost, though, the lead detectives were fortunate indeed to have obtained a written statement from the volunteer suspect; and then once booked, the alleged perpetrator's case was officially turned over to the District Attorney's Office.

From then on, it would be up to a Jury of the defendant's peers to determine if there was any chance of leniency for a person who'd shot and killed another motorist over a minor fender-bender type of accident. Yet Paul couldn't help but to quip that the suspect had better have some redeeming qualities to offer a jury if he had any hopes of staying out of prison.

From past experiences, Paul knew all too well that when a criminal case goes to trial, the arresting officer's obligation to testify in court will always be a vital and necessary responsibility that the detectives will eventually have to contend with; it simply goes with the territory.

Therefore, a successful conclusion to the road rage case was certainly good news to Paul; and especially since that he'd already made plans to spend the majority of his afternoon at the Cook County Courthouse where he was expected to testify in an old homicide case which he thought had already been resolved. The case that Paul was scheduled to testify in was one of those in which he and Ken had solved together; and even though a jury had found the defendant guilty of first degree murder, the convicted felon had since hired himself a hotshot attorney who'd just recently won a new trial for his client.

Meanwhile, Gary had planned on finishing up the day by working on the McGregor file at the stationhouse; although the detectives did make plans for the two of them to meet up on the following day for an early morning breakfast.

Then just as expected, Paul was forced to spend the majority of his afternoon by waiting in a hallway of justice for a most boring two hours before he was allowed to enjoy his fifteen minutes of fame on the witness stand. But then just as Paul was about to exit the courthouse he happened to run into one of Ken's old partners who no longer worked in homicide but was currently working out of the Missing Person's Bureau.

Then owing to the lateness of the hour, Ken's old friend, Detective Leon Hardy, hurriedly excused himself from the conversation while at the same time asking Paul to please say hello to Ken for him; but then as an afterthought Hardy stated that he'd recently found one of Paul's personal police business cards in the home of one of their missing persons.

Conversely, though, as soon as detective Hardy mentioned the name of Nurse Marie Gonzales, Paul knew that an explanation from him would be in order as to why he and Gary had been in the nurse's residence in the first place; and which was, of course, when he and Gary had first started working the old McGregor cold case. Also just as naturally, Paul queried detective Hardy as to what he believed had happened to the nurse.

"Well Paul, it's of my opinion that Nurse Gonzales has been kidnapped by her ex-husband: and I can say that with a certain amount of confidence since we've just recently learned that the missing nurse's ex-husband is not only an illegal alien, but that he's also been living off and on in Mexico ever since their divorce became final. I'm sure that you're also aware of just how difficult it is for any police department in the U. S. to extradite anyone back up here from Mexico. Therefore, that's why I believe that this case could very well end up dragging on for many years to come," detective Hardy said.

"Well Leon, good luck to you guys and I'll be sure to give Ken your message," Paul said.

Chapter Seven

Silent Witnesses

Then shortly after meeting up for their prearranged early morning breakfast at the diner on the following day, the two detectives drove directly to the stationhouse where they were planning to continue their work on the McGregor cold case. But then as Paul and Gary were making their way to the squad room coffeemaker for an early morning refill they just happened to bump into Lieutenant Oxley who asked them how their investigation on the McGregor case was progressing. But when Paul and Gary admitted that they hadn't as yet uncovered any new evidence on the cold case, the Lieutenant told them to forget about the McGregor case for a while and for them to follow him into his office.

"Someone must have had a spiritual awakening: or perhaps they had one of those deathbeds experiences of the type where they wanted to wipe the slate clean before they passed away," the Lieutenant said.

"And get this: the person who wrote this letter claims to have direct knowledge of a homicide that occurred back in nineteen hundred and sixties" the Lieutenant, said.

"I hope they're not going to confess to the shooting of our former president, John Fitzgerald Kennedy," Paul said.

For a moment, even the Lieutenant had to smile a bit, but then quickly instructed the two detectives to be sure and makes extra copies of the confessor's letter before starting a new file. So then by going on the internet, Paul easily found the website listing for the Chicago City Directory; and as luck would have it, the confessor's name and address were listed therein. Also just as luckily for the two detectives, the man had apparently been living at the same address for the past several decades.

Paul then straight away began searching the record's division for any additional information that he could find on the old homicide case which was mentioned in the letter. In the meantime, though, Gary was pulling the old cold case murder book which matched the name of the homicide case that the letter writer had referred to; then, of course, he proceeded to make copies of the most significant papers so that Paul could have something to read on the drive over to the letter writer's residence.

From time to time, it seemed as if there was never a dull moment at the stationhouse, and as if to prove the point, Paul and Gary just happened to bump in to detective Watson as they were exiting the stationhouse.

"Hey Red, where's Jackson?" Paul asked.

"Haven't you heard? Jackson asked to be transferred over to Juvenile," Watson said.

"Just imagine if you can: a six-foot six, two hundred and sixty pound monster of a man wants to be a Diaper Dick."What's the world coming to?" Paul said.

The confessor's home address was located in a wonderful part of town where if a person were to stand on a particular street corner and then look from left to right they would find pockets of Italian, Polish, and German nationalities; then too, a person would also find an Irish neighborhood thrown in for good measure. And not so surprisingly, all four of those different nationalities came together at a four-corner intersection where at first glance they appeared to form a single and indistinguishable community. However, even though the separate and individual neighborhoods appeared to be an integral part of the city, they were still somewhat separated from the rest.

Then once the detectives had arrived at the so-called confessor's residence, Paul couldn't help but think about his significant other when an attractive dark-haired woman answered the knock on the front door. Because of their normal monthly rotation, both he and Gary were up for an extended three-day weekend; and therefore, he and Evelyn had made plans to make a mini-vacation out of the weekend by traveling up to Lake Geneva, Wisconsin where they were looking forward to spending a glorious and relaxing three-day holiday.

Subsequently, then, right after the perfunctory introductions at the door had been completed, a woman named Pam escorted the two detectives to a bedroom in the rear of the house where they were introduced to an elderly gentleman who was sitting upright in a bed.

At first, Paul caught himself trying to place a face that he'd seen in the past to the name of the letter writer. Fortunately, however, he did remember to verify that the older gentleman in the bed was indeed the composer of the aforementioned letter. Although from the very beginning of the conversation it was fairly obvious to the two detectives that the woman standing guard at the foot of the older gentleman's bed would not tolerate any funny business from them; and therefore, Paul very wisely decided to speak softly while inquiring of the older man just exactly what kind information he had for them. Then after lying back comfortably on his bed, the older man said that it was going to be a long story; and so naturally, Paul and Gary immediately grabbed themselves a straight back chair.

The first clarifying statement made by the older gentleman was that the young woman standing at the foot of the bed was the daughter of his deceased brother, Eddy Colson. The elder Mr. Colson then proceeded to tell the two detectives that he was going to set them straight about what'd really happened to his brother some years ago.

"About fifteen years ago, my younger brother Eddy was indicted by a grand jury and then arrested for the murder of another bookmaker which had supposedly taken place back in the year of nineteen hundred and sixty-three. Luckily for Eddy, though, the courts failed to convict him on that charge. But from that day forward, and then all throughout the remaining days of his life, my brother swore to me on a stack of bibles that he'd not killed that bookmaking gangster. That's also around the time that he told me that not only had the police falsely accused him of committing that crime, but that they'd tried to frame him for the murder," Mr. Colson said.

"Now I'm not saying my brother was an angel, or anything like that, but I really don't think that he ever killed anybody. However, Eddy did have a few minor convictions on his police record for crimes such as bookmaking and the like; but you see, Eddy's main problem was that he wasn't a Daley man; and on top of everything else he'd very foolishly made a few enemies with the boys in blue," Mr. Colson said.

"Anyway, when Eddy passed away a few years ago, Pam here found some of his old court papers which had been stored away," Mr. Colson said.

"More importantly, though, in there amongst all of the rest of my brother's papers there was a diary in which Eddy had claimed to know the identity of the person who'd actually done the evil deed. By that I mean, Eddy claimed that he knew the name of the person who was responsible for the murder for which he'd so wrongfully been accused of committing. Gentlemen, the name of the person who killed the bookmaking gangster is listed right here in this diary along with some other very interesting reading," Mr. Colson said, as he held the diary up in the air.

"You see, Eddy lived in a constant state fear: and so naturally, when he made those entries in his diary he knew full well that he could never reveal that kind of information while he was still alive," Mr. Colson said.

"Therefore, if you two gentlemen would be kind enough to take these papers along with you, and then look into the matter, well then, we would all be mighty grateful to you," Mr. Colson said.

Thus after rising from his seat, Paul then very graciously accepted the diary from the older man while at the same time he was thanking him and Pam for their help. In the meantime, though, Gary had busied himself with the laborious job of boxing up the entire cache of paperwork. Then after once again thanking the elderly Mr. Colson and his niece Pam for their help, Paul left them one of his personal police business cards.

Then after the two detectives had carefully stored the paperwork in the trunk of their police car, Gary suggested that since it was already late Friday afternoon, and also being that the two of them were looking forward to some rest and recreation over the long weekend, he suggested that he should store the boxes of Eddy Colson's paperwork in the evidence room at the stationhouse.

And even though Paul was more than a little curious about the information that they might find in Eddy's diary, he reluctantly agreed to let Gary store the entire collection of papers in the evidence room until the following Monday morning when they would have more time to carefully assess the information. Paul then further tried to rationalize the situation by saying that since the evidence would be stored in a safe place, and also that the information listed in the paperwork was already at least fifteen years old, he certainly didn't believe that a few more days' worth of waiting would hurt anything.

All the same, it was Friday evening before Paul was finally able to make it over to Evelyn's apartment; and by then, the two of them were more than a little anxious to head north to Wisconsin where they'd already reserved a rustic little cabin which sat above the bucolic shoreline of Lake Geneva.

On the following morning, however, Paul's cell phone rang just as he and Evelyn were about to enjoy their second cup of coffee in their quaint little kitchenette. Then what happened next must have been a terribly comical situation when Paul was forced to scramble around the cabin in search of his misplaced cell phone. In the meantime, though, Evelyn had to hurriedly turn down the volume on the radio which was playing Paul's favorite rendition of, "Turn out the lights and call the Law," which was sung by Lightning Hopkins. The phone call was definitely was a stroke of bad luck for the two vacationers because Paul was then forced to tell Evelyn that a desperate situation had just come up at the stationhouse and that he'd been ordered to return to Chicago.

So primarily due to the required amount of travel time back to Chicago, it was getting along late on that Saturday afternoon before Paul was able to make it back to the stationhouse; then upon arrival, he quickly discovered that Gary was already waiting him in the squad room. It was also apparent that Lieutenant Oxley was waiting for Paul's return for just as soon as he was aware of Paul's arrival he then straight away ordered the two detectives into his office.

"What the hell's going on with you guys?" the Lieutenant asked.

"You two went out there yesterday to confirm the validity of the Colson letter that I gave you and then the first thing this morning I got a telephone call from a detective from another district who informed me that one of Mr. Colson's sons had just found two dead bodies on the inside of the Colson residence," the Lieutenant said.

"It seems that Mr. Colson and his niece were both murdered sometime during the previous evening," the Lieutenant said.

At that time, silence filled the room like heavy fog on a Shenandoah Mountain Valley floor; until, that is, when the Lieutenant finally broke the quite.

"There's another team of our detectives already on the scene so you two get your butts out there and try to find out what in the hell went wrong," the Lieutenant said.

Then just as soon as they could, Paul and Gary drove over to the scene of the crime. And even though Paul was still in a state of shock and disbelief when he entered the Colson residence, he knew from past experiences that the very first thing he needed to do was to seek out the lead detective so that he could learn the facts of the case.

The lead detective on the Colson homicide case was a policewoman by the name of Detective Sergeant Kathleen Medford who Paul knew by reputation only. However, the rumors concerning the female detective had been running rampant amongst the detectives in Paul's squad for months on end; and the scuttlebutt surrounding Kathleen Medford was that she was a stunningly beautiful woman who just happened to be blessed with a full head of gorgeous red-hair.

Though on several other occasions Paul had heard a few of the other detectives at the station make what some people might call disparaging remarks about the female detective; and one those was that Kathleen looked a lot better in a police officer's uniform blouse than she did in the business suits that she typically wore on the job. It was also a well-known fact that not only did Detective Sergeant Medford possess a beautifully proportioned, and yet full figured body, but that she was especially endowed with a set of the most spectacular breast to be found anywhere in the entire city of Chicago. Then too, it was also a well-known fact that Kathleen was far from being ashamed of her beautiful body; and as if to further augment that juicy bit of stationhouse gossip, one of the detectives in his squad had uncovered the fact that before becoming a police officer she'd worked as a model where she'd proudly displayed that gorgeous body of hers in numerous bra and panty advertisements which had appeared in various department store ads.

In due time, however, Paul was able to force his thoughts back to the work at hand: but before he could attempt to make any sense out of the whole tragic affair sergeant Medford had stepped forward. After first introducing herself, she then proceeded to inform the two detectives that the Medical Examiner had estimated the time of death of the two members of the Colson family to be somewhere around midnight past. This then meant, of course, that the murders were being committed at about the same time in the evening that he and Evelyn were thoroughly enjoying each other's company in their little cabin up in Wisconsin. Then without any further delay, Detective Sergeant Medford continued on with her explanation.

"Otherwise, Paul, except for the fact that we know the approximate time of death there's really not a whole lot more that I can tell you about the case except to say there was no forced entry and nothing of value seems to be missing from the house. Having said that, it now appears that the killer or killers might be pros; and I can say that with more than a little certainty since we have not as yet found any shell casings, fingerprints, or any other kinds of physical evidence," Detective Sergeant Medford said.

Kathleen also stated that in her opinion the double Colson homicide appeared to be a crime of revenge; but then added that she'd made that determination based solely upon the fact that each of the victims had been shot only once in the head. So on conclusion, Medford told Paul that when she sees an execution style of homicide of that nature it almost always rules out a crime of passion.

Though regardless of the outcome, Paul was well aware of the fact that the Colson case did not officially belong to him and Gary; and therefore, they decided to let the crime scene teams finish up their work and then just wait until the following Monday morning when the official reports would be made available.

DETECTIVE
CHICAGO POLICE
CITY OF CHICAGO
INCORPORATED 4th MARCH 1837
INCH
URBS IN HORTO

Chapter Eight

If you're not blue, you're through

Thus after arriving back at their stationhouse, the two detectives were still obligated to file their daily detective reports on the Colson homicide case. Although being that they were still officially off duty for the remainder of the weekend, Paul decided to call his ex-partner. Even so, when Ken finally answered the telephone, he told Paul that he was still a bit tired from having just planted some brand-new rosebushes. Regardless, though, Ken must have sensed some sort of urgency in Paul's voice because he very quickly then added that they should probably have a beer together just to celebrate the planting of the new roses.

So apart from the fact that it was already getting late on that Saturday evening before Paul was finally able to arrive at his ex-partner's home, Ken insisted that there was still ample time left in the evening for the two of them to have a beer together.

So then as quickly as he could, Paul began to mentally unload everything that was on his mind; and as he continued, he admitted to Ken that the main reason for his angst was that he was especially upset over the strange events which had taken place over at the Colson residence.

All throughout the entire conversation with Ken, Paul remembered that he'd just recently run across an old mug shot of Eddy Colson which he'd found buried in an old police file at the stationhouse. Paul stated that after seeing that old photograph of Eddy Colson he was somewhat surprised by the fact that Eddy Colson could have passed as a twin brother of the recently murdered Mr. Colson. After having said that, however, Paul made it a point to tell Ken that he hadn't shared that information with anybody at the stationhouse; including Gary.

"I do seem to remember that the Colson brothers looked more like identical twins than just mere brothers and I probably wouldn't have known that if I hadn't been in court one day when the elder Mr. Colson was testifying on behalf of his younger brother, Eddy," Ken said.

"And Ken, there's something here else too, it looks to me as if the writer of the diary, one Eddy Colson, might have been a little more involved in Organized Crime than the recently murdered older brother was willing to admit during the interview that we conducted with him yesterday; and oh by the way, our interview with the Colson family took place just hours prior to the murders which occurred later on that same evening," Paul said.

"Then too, I've just recently discovered that Eddy Colson wasn't really acquitted of the murder of that other bookmaker, but that the case was actually thrown out of court because of a technicality," Paul said.

"And Ken: guess who the lead detective on the case of the murdered bookie that Eddy Colson was accused of killing? It was Gary Materessi's Rabbi, that's who; and as you already know, Gary's Rabbi just happens to be our present-day Chief of Detectives," Paul said.

"Now wait a minute Paul, I seem to remember something about that case, or at least I heard about it later; that case started out as a righteous case but then later on it was the prosecutor who screwed that one up," Ken said.

"All right Ken, let's say for the sake of argument that you're right about the old Eddy Colson/bookmaker homicide case; but what about Gary's connection to the hospital on the night the McGregor kid got killed; and what in the hell went wrong over at the Colson residence last evening?" Paul said.

"And Ken, there's another situation that I haven't even told you about and that has to do with my bumping into your ex-partner Leon Hardy the other day when I was in court to testify on that old Stevens homicide case that you and I worked together," Paul said, and then handed Ken the envelope he'd received from Hardy.

"And speaking of Hardy, you might remember the conversation that you and I had just a few days ago when I was telling you about a woman by the name of Marie Gonzales who supposedly was a witness to the McGregor homicide. In any case, Hardy seems to think that the ex-husband might have kidnapped her and then hauled her off to Mexico; but to tell you the truth Ken, I honestly don't know just quite what to believe. For as I told you just a few days ago Nurse Gonzales was one of the first witnesses that Gary and I interviewed when we first started working the old McGregor cold case," Paul said.

"Well Paul, you certainly do seem to have a problem here all right but if you try to connect Materessi to any crime at all then you're going to need a lot of police brass on your side," Ken said.

After a few moments of silence, Paul finally spoke again.

"When you say I need a lot of brass on my side do you mean my Lieutenant and Captain?" Paul said.

"All of the above and any more you can get your hands on," Ken said.

DEAD AND COVERED UP

After thanking Ken for his help, Paul headed straight home; but then later on as he mused to himself that it'd turned out to be a real lost weekend.

CHAPTER NINE

BUILDING AN UNNATURAL CASE

The old cliché of dotting the I s and crossing the T s could be a metaphor for detective work; and especially since the bane of all investigative work comes down to not only doing the research, but by also getting the facts straight. On the other hand, though, since the advent of the modern-day computer systems, and then also with the introduction of the internet, both of these modern inventions have become powerful tools for investigators.

So within only a short period time Paul had uncovered yet another interesting fact. According to an old court record, the father of the slain McGregor lad and the present-day Chief of Detectives had at one time shared a common thread of interest. It seems that just a few years prior to the California Street Park homicide the father of the murdered McGregor boy had won a six hundred dollar civil lawsuit against a former neighbor of his; and interestingly enough, the loser of the lawsuit just happened to be a police officer who would later climb up the ranks of the police department to eventually hold the position of Chief of Detectives. So what's the big deal here? Paul thought. What the heck, it was only a measly six hundred dollar loss, right.

However, when Paul began trying to put all the missing pieces of the puzzle together he realized that he knew just two seminal facts for certain. One of those was the fact that Gary Materessi was working at the Hospital on the very same evening that the McGregor lad was killed; and secondly, that Gary had been interviewed at the crime scene by O'Riley.

By then, Paul had begun to suspect that his partner, Gary Materessi, had a long-standing hero-worship fixation on the Chief of Detectives. Consequently, Paul's theory of Gary's complicity in the murder of the McGregor youth was looking a lot more believable when on the following Monday morning he went into the evidence room at the stationhouse to retrieve Eddy Colson's diary but then found that the entire Colson file had mysteriously disappeared.

Paul's suspicion of Gary had begun to increase even more significantly when he found an old in-house police report showing that Gary Materessi was one of the primary investigators on the old bookmaker/Eddy Colson homicide case. Then too, Paul discovered that Gary had also worked the bookmaker/homicide case both before and during the same time that Eddy Colson was standing trial.

Hence, as a direct result of his intensive research work, Paul uncovered the fact that detective Gary Materessi was the first police officer to have arrived on the scene when the bookmaker Eddy Colson was found dead. Then after doing some more investigative work, Paul discovered that Gary had stated in one of his incident reports that he'd arrived just shortly after a train had run over and killed Eddy Colson. Eventually though, Paul discovered that Gary had written most of the official police incident reports concerning the peculiar case of Eddy Colson's accident/suicide.

What Paul had found most intriguing about the death of Eddy Colson was that it'd been ruled an accident and that determination in and of itself had seemed especially interesting to Paul since detective Materessi was the only eyewitness on the scene. So in addition to Gary's personal involvement in the death of Eddy Colson, and then along with all the rest of the incriminating circumstantial evidence which was rapidly mounting against him, one determining factor stood out alone; and that simply was the statement that Gary had made in his final report where he avowed that he was the only other person standing on the train platform when Eddy Colson allegedly fell or jumped in front of one of the fast moving El Trains.

Consequently, then, with no other eyewitnesses to the alleged accident, with the exception of Gary Materessi, that is, Eddy Colson's death had to either be ruled an accident, or else it had to be adjudged a case of suicide.

The longer Paul worked in homicide the more fervently he believed in an external source of evil; although a quote he'd once read might dispute that theory since it stated that, "The belief in a supernatural source of evil is not necessary; men alone are quite capable of every wickedness."

So then after feeling that he'd collected more than enough circumstantial evidence against Materessi to at least warrant further investigation, Paul asked for, and received, a Union Representative to appear with him in a meeting with the brass. Not only would the meeting include both his Lieutenant and Captain, but it would also include a representative from the Internal Affairs Division.

However, since that the Chief of Detective's name had come up during his extensive investigation, Paul felt that it would also be prudent to ask the Deputy Chief of Detectives to attend the meeting as well.

Then notwithstanding the Chicago Police Department's prerogative to conduct its own internal investigation, the brass immediately ordered Paul into the main police headquarters; and after being admitted into the inner sanctum of the Chief's office Paul was told that Materessi had been arrested on multiple counts of suspicion of murder.

Then later on, but only after the police department's own psychiatrists had been given the opportunity to more thoroughly examine Materessi, they discovered that Gary had suffered a complete psychotic break. Unfortunately, however, none of the brass at the main police headquarters could explain to Paul just exactly how the good doctors had missed the presence of Gary's mental illness during the initial policeman's application process.

There were, however, more than a few people in the department who bravely stated that there's always a possibility that certain parts of the prospective patrolman's examination had been deliberately bypassed.

And as unfortunate as it may be, there's always a possibility that a directive from someone high-up in the police department, or even someone in city hall, could have easily gotten Materessi's application approved.

Then too, there was always another possibility: and that simply was that someone high-up in the department had kissed and then cosigned Materessi's application in order to pay off an old political debt. In that worst case scenario, a situation of that nature would have almost certainly guaranteed that Materessi would have been hired regardless of any of the other test results.

But be that as it may, when Materessi appeared in court for his initial hearing on the multiple counts of homicide, the lead prosecutor for State of Illinois boldly stated that the prosecutor's office intended to prove that Gary Materessi, and not Eddy Colson, had killed the bookmaking gangster.

Moreover, when the rest of the facts of the case were eventually made public, the prosecutors announced that they planned on proving that Gary Materessi was responsible for the murders of the McGregor lad, Mr. Colson, and Eddy Colson's daughter, Pam. In the case of Nurse Marie Gonzales, however, the head of the Bureau of Missing Persons Division declared that the case would be considered an active file.

To Paul, the most satisfying result of the entire investigation was that no incriminating evidence was ever found against the Chief of Detectives; for it was determined that the chief was totally unaware of the Machiavellian types of shenanigans which were being practiced by Materessi. Therefore, when the whole truth of the matter was known publicly it was beneficial to everybody at police headquarters.

In his heart of hearts, Paul sincerely believed that Materessi would have been willing to do almost anything to protect his patron and friend, the Chief of Detectives. And as unfortunate as it may be, Materessi had become a Zealot; then again, everybody knows that the main problem with Zealots is that they always think that they're right; and unfortunately, they also sincerely believe that they're always on the side of God. It was all a bit too surreal for Paul but it was just another day at the office.

DETECTIVE
CHICAGO POLICE
CITY OF CHICAGO
INCORPORATED 4th MARCH 1837

VICE AND VIRTUE

CHAPTER ONE

THE INDOCTRINATION

After being promoted to the rank of detective, Mathew Morris would represent the fourth generation of his family to have served on the Chicago Police Department as a homicide detective. The Morris family of Chicago had a longstanding tradition of producing excellent and dedicated law enforcement officers which began in the nineteen twenties when Mathew's great-grandfather, James Morris, became the first member of the Morris family to serve on the Chicago Police Department as a homicide detective; and James was especially proud of the role that he'd played as the lead detective on the St. Valentine's Day Massacre case.

Mathew's Grandfather, Peter Morris, had also been a highly decorated detective but he was best noted for the solving of a nineteen-fifties era multiple homicide case that was known at the time as the "Dumpster Case."

Back in the nineteen nineties, Mathew's Father, Paul Morris, was instrumental in the solving of the murder of a famous Chicago Cub's baseball player; and in addition to his involvement in that one spectacular case, Paul had aided the Chicago Police Department in ridding itself of a psychotic homicide detective.

As they say, change is inevitable, and after having worked out of the Chicago Police Department's Homicide Division for a period of several years detective Mathew Morris, and his partner William Margent, were more than a little surprised to learn that they were about to be temporarily assigned to the Chicago Police Department's Gang Unit.

This somewhat unexpected transfer to an entirely different squad was decided upon by the Chief of Detectives who'd made the decision in an attempt to try to stem the steady rise of gang activity which had been increasing at an alarming rate.

The incidence of gang violence was certainly nothing new to the members of the Chicago Police Department's Gang Unit who'd been dealing with the scourge of organized crime since the days of prohibition, and even well before then.

Although in Matt's way of thinking about the only real difference that he could see in the makeup of the gangs of old and the modern-day gangs is just the ethnicity of their membership; then too, Matt knew full well that the love of money has always been, and always will be the primary reason for their existence.

Then once officially transferred over to the gang unit, Matt knew that the homicides he would be asked to investigate in the future would be a little different in their nature as compared to the types cases he'd previously handled while working primarily out of the Homicide Division; and which were, of course, the kinds of murders which are usually associated with the crimes of passion, and/or, armed robbery.

In the years that Matt had been on the force he thought he'd seen more than his fair share of violence and mayhem; but then after having personally witnessed some of the terrible results of the modern-day turf wars which were currently taking place between two of the city's most violent and ruthless gangs he could see that he would have to steel himself even further against the inevitability of what could only be called mass murder.

The two groups of thugs with which the detectives of the gang unit were primarily concerned with were known as the Black Gangster Disciples; with one of the groups holding reign on the Southside of the city while the other one is invested mainly in the Westside of town.

However, that's certainly not to say that a few of the other local gangs, such as the Vice Lords, which happens to be the oldest gang in the city of Chicago, or even a few of the other the gangs such as El Rukin and the Black Stone Rangers haven't also been responsible for their share of the violence and mayhem.

Though here of late, an unexpected and a much welcomed ray of hope had suddenly loomed large in the future of the African American youth of Chicago when a man by the name of Leonard Brown claimed to have found religion and has since retired from the life of crime.

Then too, it was also a well-known fact to the members of the gang unit that just prior to Mr. Leonard Brown's wise decision to quit the life of crime and violence he was better known to the police by the street name of Bad Leroy; and not so surprisingly, it's been said that Mr. Brown had chosen that particular street name because he especially enjoyed being identified with the character in the song by the name of, "Bad-Bad Leroy Brown."

And just like the Leroy of song and verse, Mr. Leonard Brown had also hailed from the Southside of Chicago where he'd striven to be just like the Leroy

Brown of song who was said to have been the "Baddest man in the whole damn town".

Accordingly, then, we are only left to assume that a monumental spiritual awakening must have been the driving force behind the aforementioned gentleman's sudden conversion. There were, however, more than a few people in the city of Chicago who suspected that the main reason behind Mr. Leonard Brown's wise decision to retire from the life of gang-banging was primarily due to the fact that he'd already been shot eight times; and therefore, they were prone to suspect that Mr. Brown's newly found religion was only a minor consideration.

Moreover, some of those same people have also stated that since Mr. Leonard Brown had already been shot eight times, then there was always the possibility that he might have felt as if his life was similar to that of the proverbial cat of myth and legend in as much as he was now living his ninth and final life on this good earth.

Nonetheless, one of the most amazing aspects of Mr. Brown's newly morphed persona was the fact that not only had he managed to live long enough to celebrate his thirty-fifth birthday, but that he'd also managed to stay out of prison; and those two factors alone had helped to impel Leroy's sparkling new image into that of a modern-day superhero type of figure.

At the end of the day though, and who amongst us could really blame him, Leroy decided that he might as well cash in on his now famous name by writing an expose' type of book in which he detailed the life of a Chicago (Gangsta). And upon publication, not too many people were surprised when Leroy's book had not only become an instant bestseller in the city of Chicago, but the book had become enormously popular around the rest of the country as well. To his credit, however, Leroy the author has continued to celebrate his newfound success and notoriety by working tirelessly with the various local Neighborhood Youth Improvement Associations throughout the city of Chicago.

DETECTIVE
CHICAGO POLICE
CITY OF CHICAGO
INCORPORATED 4th MARCH 1837
213

Chapter Two

Learning the Ropes

For as many years as some people would care to remember, and this goes all of the back to the early days of prohibition, the gang unit has been an invaluable source of information for the detectives who work out of the Chicago Police Department's Homicide Division. Accordingly, then, the homicide detectives are just naturally pleased when one of their gang unit's (P Is), or personal informants, comes forward with some vital information concerning any present-day gang activity for which they're willing to either trade for, or even to sell to a member of the Chicago Police Department.

Generally speaking, however, information of that type is usually only relevant to the detectives in the gang unit for just a short period of time; and that's primarily due to the fact that the average lifespan of an active gang member is almost always cut short by either a long stint in prison, or even worse, they can just as easily end up in a cemetery.

Nevertheless, the gang unit detectives can only hope and pray that some of the information they're able to glean from their informants might end up being useful to the homicide detectives who're actively working a murder where upon first glance the case appears to be unsolvable.

At the end of the day, though, both Matt Morris and his partner, Bill Margent, came to the conclusion that if they ever had any hopes of solving any one of the gang related homicides that they'd just recently been assigned then they would first need the help of someone on the inside; and so naturally, they decided that what they needed most was the expertise and knowledge of the man who was formally known as Bad Leroy Brown.

So fortunately for Matt and Bill's sake, their plan of having a sit-down meeting with the ex-gangster was most eagerly accepted by their supervisor in the gang unit, Lieutenant Steven Morgan, who wholeheartedly agreed with them that they should definitely attempt to turn Mr. Brown into a police informant.

So in due time, a meeting between Chicago's latest bestselling author, and the two former homicide detectives, was not only agreed upon but was immediately scheduled to take place at one of the stationhouses on the Southside of town.

However, any hopes of a successful outcome were suddenly dashed when Mr. Brown showed up for the meeting and claimed to have no personal knowledge whatsoever of any of the gang related murders, past or present.

Of course, Matt and Bill were a tad bit disappointed with Mr. Brown for the way in which the meeting had turned out, but they considered his refusal to help as only a minor setback; and as such, they weren't in the least dissuaded from trying to attain their goal which was to quell the present-day slaughter. For in Matt's way of thinking it simply meant that they would now have to find a completely new and different way to come up with the intelligence they so desperately needed in order to further themselves along in the investigations of the multiple homicide cases that they were currently working.

The one case in particular that the two detectives were most interested in solving was a cold case which had occurred back in the year of nineteen hundred and ninety-four when a fourteen year old gang member, who went by the street name of Yummy, was killed execution style by his own associates; and at the time of the murder the word on the street was that the young boy had been killed because the leaders of his own gang had mistakenly believed that he'd become an informant for the Chicago Police Department.

And even though the murderous gang-members would eventually come to realize that they'd made a terrible mistake by killing the wrong person, the murder of the young boy has since made it much more difficult for anyone on the police department to be able to convince any of the other gang members, or even the public at large for that matter, to give evidence in court against any of the active gang members.

So to Matt and Bill, it was perfectly clear that they would have to travel down a completely different path if they ever had any hopes of solving any one of the gang-related homicide cases that they'd just recently caught.

Yet on one unparticular day, as Matt was reflecting back on all of the homicide cases that he'd worked in the past, he just happened to remember that very little in life had ever come easy for him; albeit, he also knew that it was primarily due to the nature of his work.

On the other hand, though, Matt's greatest modern-day dilemma was simply how best to infiltrate one of the gangs. Of course Matt was also aware of the fact that just the act of trying to convince an active gang member to flip, or to rollover on his associates, has always been a very difficult task for anybody in the law enforcement community to accomplish; then again, the solving of any homicide case can at times be a very complex issue.

Nowadays, however, in addition to owning the age-old responsibility of having to solve crimes, there's a new trend in law enforcement that places a greater emphasis on the prevention of crime; but then as everybody on the job already knows, it's almost impossible to prevent the crime of murder; and that seems to be especially true in cities the size of Chicago where the respective police departments certainly don't have the available manpower to put an officer on every street corner. Plus in addition to the lack of manpower, the city of Chicago also doesn't have the tens of thousands of cameras installed on the vital intersections like the city of London, England has.

Therefore, the majority of all the murders that routinely take place in a city the size of Chicago are still solved the old fashioned way; and which then means that it still requires a lot hard work and skill on the part of the homicide detectives.

Although that's certainly not to imply that the relatively new science of genetics and D. N. A. evidence hasn't been a tremendous help to the various law enforcement agencies spread out across the country; but then regardless of how much of a benefit the D. N. A. evidence might be to the prosecutors who're charged with convicting the killers, the police must first identify the suspected guilty parties before they can even be arrested and brought into court.

Chapter Three

Devising a Plan

So with the present-day crackdown on gang activity well underway, there certainly weren't any shortages of suspects for the two detectives to interview; and the questioning of a homicide suspect is where Matt seems to do his best work.

Generally speaking, any time that Matt is presented with the opportunity to interview a suspect he almost always prefers to conduct the session in the same manner that his father had taught him; and that's usually accomplished by employing a simple method of interrogation whereby the investigator begins the interview by asking the suspect a few poignant and personal questions about themselves.

Though more than once, Matt's father has suggested to him that he should always try to listen very carefully to what the suspects might have to say. More importantly, however, he taught Matt that he must also be on his guard when interrogating a person of interest since the majority of suspects will invariably try to talk about everything under the sun except for the main reason that they're sitting in an interrogation room in the first place. So in Matt's way of looking at things his father's technique of questioning a person of interest has proved to be the correct way; and especially since the suspects are just naturally a little nervous when they're being questioned by the police.

In addition to coaching his son on how to become a better listener, Matt's father had taught him that he should always try to make the interview seem a little more personal to the suspect by making a statement similar to the following, "We already know that your partner's girlfriend's name is so and so." Then notwithstanding the probability of the suspect's failure to recognize the subterfuge and psychology which had just been employed by the detective, the suspect might even correct the detective's mistake; and by doing so, he or she might just give up some valuable information.

Just the act of being able to get a person of interest to speak openly and freely to a police officer is in and of itself an art which normally requires a lot of experience. And even though some of the old-time detectives still prefer to use the rough approach when dealing with their suspects, some of the more modern-day detectives, like Matt, feel as though they're more successful in the long run when using the soft touch.

So all throughout the years, Matt has found through trial and error what works best for him; and therefore, his favorite method of interrogating a suspect is to put all of his cards on the table and then just sit back while nodding his head with that all-knowing expression on his face while the primary suspect continues on with his or her obvious lies and alibi's. Then again, no one system works all of the time; and that old axiom seems to be especially true nowadays since the detectives in those made for T. V. police and crime shows almost always advise their suspects that all they have to do is to, "lawyer-up."

At that point in time, however, things just weren't going all that well for Matt and Bill; as a matter of fact, they were beginning to feel stymied in their quest to find the people who were responsible for any one of the gang related murders that they were currently investigating. Therefore, it was beginning to look as if they might even have to start over from scratch if they had any plans on solving the murder of the young man with the nickname of Yummy. To the detectives, it was obvious that a different approach was definitely called for; and especially since the now famous author, Leonard Brown, had let them down by claiming to have what Matt preferred to call selective amnesia.

Accordingly, then, both Matt and Bill had come to realize that the only real chance they would ever have of solving any one of their assigned homicide cases was for them to somehow find a way to get inside the minds of the city's two most notorious gang leaders. For by then, the detectives were convinced that the two gang leaders in question were most likely responsible for the majority of all the latest gang related homicides in the city of Chicago.

Even so, the detectives felt as if they were somewhat fortunate in the sense that the two gang leaders wouldn't be all that difficult to locate and especially since one of them had just recently been busted for carrying a handgun without a permit; and which then made Matt wonder, "why in the world would a well-known gangster ever be stupid enough to get caught carrying a firearm illegally."

And even though Matt had always been interested in the science of psychology, he has never fully subscribed to the Peter Principal Theory which states in part that many of our great American institutions, including business, industry, academia, politics, and even the clergy, are basically shocked full of incompetence; but then after having personally witnessed some of the stupid acts which are routinely carried out by the so-called masterminds of the criminal elements, Matt had come to realize that he might have to rethink his stance on that score.

Matt knew, of course, that the weapons charge case for which the gang leader had just recently been busted could very well end up being very problematic for the gang leader; and particularly since the state of Illinois has some of the toughest modern-day gun laws on the books to be found anywhere in the entire country. Moreover, the Illinois State gun laws are so all-encompassing that they mandate that even some of the firearms which are usually legal if kept in one's own home must now be duly registered with their respective police departments.

At times, the stringent new gun laws can be very beneficial to the people in law enforcement; then again, the laws can be doubly unfortunate for the criminal elements who unwisely decide to take up residence in the state of Illinois.

Furthermore, since Matt is always looking for an edge anyway, his new way of thinking was that Gilford Minton's recent arrest for carrying a concealed weapon without a permit might just possibly give him and Bill a little added leverage that they could use against the notorious gang leader.

So at that point in time it seemed only natural for Matt and Bill to begin looking for even more creative ways to bring down two of the city's most violent gang leaders; and even though Gilford Minton was much better known for making his fortunes from the fruits of his various criminal activities, he has almost certainly learned from the mistakes of his predecessors, such as Al Capone, who was taken down for failure to pay his taxes.

Therefore, the vast majority of all the modern-day gangsters have come to understand the necessity for criminals of their stature to own at least a few legitimate businesses just so they could not only launder their dirty money, but that they would also have a way to in which prove to the various government agencies that they could afford to live in such a luxurious lifestyle.

So in addition to owning a number of other legitimate businesses, Gilford Minton had somehow found the time to run a restaurant on the Southside of town which was known primarily for serving the Southern Style of cooking; but then along with the home-style plate lunches that Mr. Minton's restaurant offers, his café was forced to serve the standard fare of hotdogs, hamburgers and pizza which to this day are still hugely popular with many of the younger people.

Nonetheless, the investigators were about to come face to face with yet another dilemma and that was simply how best to get close to their prey. For even though they knew that Minton was purported to be the owner of the restaurant, they also knew that just the act of infiltrating a gangster's operation can at times be very difficult.

Then luckily for the two detectives, Matt just happened to be a lot younger than many of the other detectives in their squad; and therefore, he felt as if he might just hold a slight edge over some of the older detectives who at first blush might not see the need for a police department to have access to the information highway.

Though just prior to his transfer to the gang unit, Matt had mistakenly believed that just the act of getting to know the two leaders of the gangs would prove to be a monumental task. In reality, though, locating of the gangsters had actually turned out to be a slam-dunk; for as it happened, Matt discovered that all of the businesses which are allowed to operate within the city limits of Chicago are required by law to obtain a permit from the

Cook County Courthouse; and therefore, the owner's names and addresses were listed on the tax rolls.

Of course the experienced detectives already know that any investigation into the present will almost always begin with a visit to the past; therefore, when Matt and Bill were still in the early stages of investigating the various legitimate businesses that Mr. Minton purportedly owned, they just naturally had the opportunity to view a few copies of his old mug-shots. Then as Matt was reviewing some of the secretly filmed police videotapes of the gangster known as Gilford Minton, he couldn't help but quip that Mr. Minton must serve a lot of good food in his café since the restaurant owner appears to weigh close to three hundred pounds.

So from that point in time it was straight away decided that a meeting of the minds was definitely called for; and so their immediate plan was for them to show up unannounced at Mr. Minton's restaurant for an early morning get-together.

Thus after arriving at the establishment that was supposedly owned by Minton, and also being that it was the first time that the two detectives had ever had the opportunity to meet the notorious gangster in person, they noticed that Gilford Minton seemed to be a pleasant enough of a person to converse with; then again, it might have just seemed that way since they were meeting the man in a social setting instead of the way in which they usually get to know a person of interest; and which would be, of course, in an interrogation room at one of the district's stationhouses.

Even so, after having spent only a few minutes with the well-known mobster, the two detectives came to the realization that Mr. Minton wasn't exactly what one might want to call the talkative type. Moreover, he didn't appear to be even a little bit rattled when Matt mentioned the name of the restaurateur's pre-sentencing probation officer that the court had assigned to him because of the fairly recent concealed weapons charge.

Although during their conversation with Minton, Matt just happened to remember something that his father had once told him about how best to handle a suspect during an informal type of interrogation; and that very simply was that it's sometimes wiser to let your person of interest assume that you have more information and evidence at your disposal than you actually have.

So while Matt was attempting to apply that practical and useful investigative tool to the situation at hand, he quickly decided that in addition to telling Minton about the conversation that he and Bill had just had with (Bad Leroy) Leonard Brown, he would suggest to Mr. Minton that Mr. Brown had mentioned his name; and which wasn't really true, of course, but to Matt's way of thinking, "all's fair in love, war, and crime".

Even so, after hearing such an inciting statement which had purportedly come from the former gang leader, Leonard Brown, Minton's composer and deportment had suddenly changed for the worse. Then apparently without thinking any too clearly Minton said, "Rather than just sitting around and writing those expose` types of books it might be best if Bad Leroy found a different line of work; or better yet, perhaps he should just leave town."

More importantly, though, no sooner had Minton spoken those words aloud then did he realize that he'd just made a monumental mistake by losing his temper in front of Matt and Bill; and then as if to somehow lessen the damage he'd just caused by running his mouth he instinctively flashed that beautiful white smile of his while at the same time saying, "Don't you just love reformed whores."

Also luckily for Matt, he then remembered something else that his father had once told him about business in general and that was, "If you want to know something about any given company, or even its manager, then you probably shouldn't be wasting your time by talking to the employees who still work for that particular organization; instead, it might be far wiser if you had a word with the people who no longer work there; or better yet, you might want to talk to some of the people who work for one of their competitors."

So expressly because of that one singular and logical line of reasoning the two detectives decided that it would behoove them to have a word with a certain Mr. Tim Bolton who was known by the dicks in the Narcotic's Division to be Mr. Minton's number one competitor in the illegal drug trade.

CHAPTER FOUR

PART TWO OF THE PLAN

According to the detectives in Vice, Tim Bolton was purported to be the leader of one of the most violent gang in the entire city of Chicago; and in addition to all of the other businesses that he allegedly owned, some legitimate and some not, he still somehow found the time to manage a small bar on the Westside of town; so therefore, the very next thing on Matt and Bill's list of things to do that day was to pay Mr. Bolton a little visit at his tavern in hopes that he would be in attendance.

On that particular day, Lady Luck was apparently with the two detectives for no sooner had they entered Mr. Bolton's mostly unlit bar, then the alleged gangster began walking straight towards them. Surprisingly, though, the very first thing that Matt noticed about the well-known gangster was that he seemed to glide effortlessly across the floor with almost feathery like legs; this then meant to Matt that the owner of the bar was most likely a jogger like he himself was.

But then the next thing Matt couldn't help but notice, besides the darkened interior of the building, was that the music coming from the jukebox was extremely loud, and that seemed somewhat strange since it was just barely eleven o'clock in the morning.

As a rule, Matt didn't harbor any real fear for his personal safety when he was forced to enter one of the gang's known hangouts; and that was primarily due to the fact that the majority of the C. P D. Officers who'd been slain on the job had either been killed when they were serving an arrest warrant, or else, they were just simply conducting a routine traffic stop. Though generally speaking, the two most dangerous situations that a police officer faces on a daily basis will occur mostly when they're either responding to a domestic call for help, or else when they're faced with a robbery in progress.

Though to this day, Matt still has some vivid memories of an injury he'd once sustained while working out of one of the uniform divisions. That particular case in point had come about when after he and his partner had responded to a domestic disturbance at one of the city's low-income high-rises; and in the ensuing melee`, Matt was struck on the back of the head with an iron skillet by the very same woman who just moments earlier had asked the officers to haul the drunken husband off to jail.

In the not too far distant past, however, there have been a few instances where a Chicago Police Officer was gunned down from ambush; and not so surprisingly, those singular types of incidents have almost always taken place when the officers were either sitting in their patrol cars, or they were just simply walking their beats.

Then as if to make matters even worse, those isolated cases from the past have since made it almost impossible for the police officers of today to be able to safely walk their beats while in uniform; and that situation seems to be especially true on the Southside of town where if the officers are lucky then only a team of detectives might feel safe enough to venture outside their car without having to call dispatch for assistance. Even so, the detectives can only get away with a ruse of that type on certain limited occasions; and even then, that's most likely because the people on the streets are never quite sure if the "suits" are really "the man," or if they're just two more of the local big-time drug dealers. Then also just as surprisingly, it can actually be safer for a white police officer to appear on the streets of a predominately black neighborhood than it is for a black policeman to do so and that's primarily because of their fear of being called an, "Uncle Tom."

Furthermore, and as unfortunate as it may be, the fear of anarchy in the city streets of Chicago has since prompted many of today's uniformed police officers to leave their loaded backup pistols lying on the seats of their patrol cars where they would be readily available if needed.

Having said that, all throughout the years that Matt had been on the job he has seldom felt it necessary to call in for assistance. Albeit, during those times when Matt has needed help from his fellow officers there was never any doubt in his mind that the streets would immediately be filled with the Squad-Roll Patty Wagons; and on one particular occasion, dispatch took it upon themselves to order in one of those large blue police busses that can deliver up to at least two dozen uniformed policemen to the scene of the disturbance.

Though in recent times, Matt has noticed a general trend towards the more flagrant assaults upon the law enforcement officers who serve the city of Chicago; and consequently, Matt fervently believes that the main reason behind the escalation of the current violence towards the police is primarily due to the fact that the majority of the police departments across the country are now much more fully aware of the need to protect the fundamental civil rights of the citizens that they've been hired to "Protect and to Serve."

Then too, Matt is also well aware of the fact that we're definitely not still living back in the nineteen forties and fifties when the police officers across the nation were more apt to use excessive force. Even so, Matt believes that the criminal elements in the city of Chicago still have a healthy respect for, and perhaps even a slight fear of the C. P. D.

So without missing a beat in the conversation that they were having with the gangster Bolton, Matt was somehow able to bring his thoughts back to the business at hand as he and Bill continued on with their questioning of Mr. Bolton, who after learning that the dialogue they were having almost wholly concerned another person's interest wasn't a bit too shy about talking. And when asked, Bolton acknowledged that he too had read Bad Leroy's book; but then not so surprisingly Bolton stated that in his opinion Bad Leroy's book was not only a great piece of literature, but that it smacked of having been written with a Shakespearean quality.

Also luckily for Matt, he remembered the old adage of, "All's fair in Love and War;" and so after reaching down deeply into his bag of interrogation tricks, he told Bolton that Gilford Minton had just said that he was all washed up. Of course, Minton hadn't actually made that statement but since the two detectives were in the midst of investigating several different gang-related homicides they felt that they should be able to use almost any ruse they deemed necessary as long as it helped them to solve their cases.

To be sure, Matt's plan to upset his quarry was apparently working as intended for when he mentioned Gilford Minton's name Mr. Bolton appeared to have suddenly experienced a drastic mood change; and which in turn had led him to state foolishly that the word on the street was that both Leonard Brown and Gilford Minton might live a little longer if only they could learn to keep their big mouths shut.

And even though Matt didn't expect to get an honest answer from the gangster, he nonetheless decided upon a completely different type of approach by asking the hoodlum what he knew about the latest gang related homicide which had just recently taken place on the Southside.

At first, it appeared as if Bolton was planning to feign complete ignorance on the subject; instead, though, he surprised the two detectives by saying that even though he didn't personally know the identities of the shooters, the word on the street was that the latest shooting was similar to the situation which had taken place back in ninety-four when a young boy by the name Yummy was murdered by his own people. Furthermore, or at least according to Bolton, that almost surely meant that the unfortunate death of the young man had not only been ordered by Gilford Minton, but that the killing had most likely been carried out by the dead gang member's own set, or his associate gang members.

So naturally, an accusatory statement of that nature coming from a rival gang leader such as Bolton almost immediately set Matt to thinking that he and Bill were going to have start eating a lot more of Gilford Minton's Southern Style cooking if they had any hopes of obtaining the information that they so desperately needed in order to solve any of the homicides cases that they were currently working.

In the past, anytime that Matt felt that he was stumped by a case, or even when he felt as though he needed help the most, it seemed as if something would almost always appear magically out of nowhere. Consequently, then, as the two detectives were making the drive over to the Southside of town where Minton's restaurant was located, help suddenly appeared. Then not too surprisingly, the badly needed help would came from his partner who just happened to remember an old tidbit of intelligence that he'd once garnered while he was still working out one of the uniform divisions.

"After working out the Southside District for a period of several years I just naturally became somewhat familiar with a few of the local drug dealers; and even though I never had the opportunity to get to know any of them personally I did have the chance to befriend one of the guys in the district, who after experiencing a few run-ins with the law, has since gone straight," Bill said.

"It sounds to me as if he's the person that we should to be talking to", Matt said.

Then as Bill continued with his recollections from the past, he told Matt that the man he was referring to was known throughout the Southside as the "Detail Man," and that the man had earned that unusual moniker because he now runs an automobile repair shop that specializes in the detailing of cars.

"And Matt, it's a well-known fact that not only does Jimmy Wagner, a/k/a the detail man detail the cars for the people who drive the late model cars, but that his preferred list of customers includes many of the big-time drug dealers," Bill said.

Thus as Bill continued to expand on the details concerning the man named Jimmy, he told Matt that the word on the streets was that the detail man was able to procure the drug dealer's automobile business because, he too, had at one been a major drug dealer; and consequently, the dealers felt as though they could count on him to keep his mouth shut.

Hence, the next thing on their list of things to do that day was to pay the ex-con a little visit. Then upon entering the detail man's shop, the man known as Jimmy just naturally addressed Bill as officer Margent. But then of course Matt had to correct the detail man's mistake by telling him that Bill's proper title nowadays was detective Margent, and that his name was detective Morris.

Though at that point in time Bill could only guess as to which interrogation technique his senior partner was planning to use on the ex-drug dealer. So notwithstanding the familiarity that they had of each other when it comes to interviewing suspects, it was soon apparent to Bill that Matt had made the conscious decision to abandon all pretenses of tact and diplomacy; and instead, he then very straightforwardly and bluntly asked Jimmy just exactly what he knew about the man named Gilford Minton.

Generally speaking, however, if a person were to judge the situation by simply looking at the stunned appearance on the detail man's face, then an outsider might think that Matt had just rapped him squarely on the top of his head with a nightstick. For just the mention of Minton's name had caused Bill's old acquaintance to suddenly assume a very solemn expression; and for a moment or two, it appeared that he might actually be planning to clam up on them.

Instead, however, he not only acknowledged that Minton was a good customer of his but that he'd just recently detailed the man's Cadillac. Then shortly thereafter, Jimmy told the detectives that he didn't wish to talk about Minton anymore because the man in question was definitely a bad dude. "It's like this, I can get into big trouble by just talking to you guys," Jimmy said.

So regardless of the fact that Matt had nothing but feelings of empathy toward the man named Jimmy, and his well-grounded fear of the drug lords, the situation had at least provided the two detectives with the opportunity to act out the age-old strategy of good cop and bad cop.

On the other hand, though, Bill was keenly aware of the fact that he and Matt had already placed Jimmy in a precarious position by just being there at the shop; so therefore, he then very discreetly slipped the detail man one of his personal police business cards. In the meantime, Matt had begun to yell very loudly at the ex-con. Then at one point in the charade Matt even went so far as to threaten Jimmy with the possibility of an arrest; but then of course, all that had been done for show. In fact, the entire scene had been played out for the sole benefit of the detail man's helper who'd been watching and listening from afar.

So then following their superb acting job at the detail man's shop, the two detectives headed on back to the stationhouse where the very next thing on Matt's agenda that day would be to return a phone call to a person that he only vaguely remembered but who was a person that he'd apparently met while investigating an old homicide case. And fortunately for Matt, he'd already been pre-schooled by his father on how best to handle a situation of that type; and which basically is that a person from the past, or even the present, will invariably contact a police officer with a request for them to use their influence to help someone out of an unpleasant situation.

And even though Matt had faithfully promised the man from the past that he would indeed look into the matter, he decided that instead of getting involved in the mess that it would be far wiser for him to handle the request for assistance in as much the same fashion as he usually does when faced with a similar type of situation; and that would be to do absolutely nothing at all.

Matt secretly suspected that he might be guilty of trying to rationalize his own actions for throughout the years he'd noticed that the punishment that's usually meted out by the courts on the majority of the criminal cases of which he'd personally been involved in have almost always been reduced in severity by their own initiative. That is, once the overworked and overloaded prosecutors have had a chance to more fully review the merits of the pending case, then there's a very good likelihood that the charges will be reduced. Therefore, the citizen who makes the initial phone call to a policeman for help would just naturally think that the officer had actually gone to bat for them when in all actuality the officer hadn't lifted a finger to help.

In due time, Matt was finally able to get off the telephone with the person who'd called for his assistance; and then once free, Bill immediately then interrupted his thoughts by saying that he wished they'd had the chance to inspect Minton's car before it'd been detailed. Though from past experiences Matt knew that if there were any traces of blood to be found anywhere in Minton's car then it probably still wasn't too late for the police technicians to find the evidence.

Nowadays, it seems that a person doesn't have to be a policeman to know some of the tricks of the trade; for even the civilians who watch television are fully aware of the fact that the real life police crime scene investigators will regularly use a chemical by the name of luminol which can detect even trace amounts of human blood on almost any material; and in some situations, the techs can find minute vestiges of blood evidence even well after the materials have been thoroughly cleaned.

So by then, both Matt and Bill were in full agreement that the very next goal they needed to accomplish would be to somehow find a way to get a close look at the interior of Minton's car. However, they also knew that if they had any hopes of convincing their Lieutenant of the need for a search warrant that would allow them to impound the gang leader's car, they would first have to come up with some hard evidence. Though at the present time it looked as if the possibility of them ever being able to uncover any additional evidence against Minton was slim and none.

On the following morning, however, the detectives were about to catch an exceptional break in their case against Minton; and this fortunate stroke of luck came about when Bill remembered that Gilford Minton had an impending court date on the concealed weapons charge for which the detectives could only hope and pray that it might just be their ace in the hole. "Guns on Parole," Bill proudly exclaimed, while smiling broadly at Matt for having just remembered one of law enforcement's most favored and preferred ways in which the boys in blue can take a bad boy off the streets.

Then, since it was part of their normal daily routine to do so, the two detectives began to playact their old game of what if and plan B which was really nothing more than a procedure they sometimes used which was accomplished by their asking one another a question for which they knew they had no rational answer. And even though the practice was seldom if ever really helpful in the solving of a homicide case, it was just another investigating tool that they sometimes used whenever they ran into a juggernaut such as the predicament that they currently found themselves facing.

Happily, though, the two detectives were about to receive another incredible break in their case against the gang leader when Matt asked Bill to run Minton's name through the Department of Motor Vehicle's data base just so they would then have the correct make, model, and license plate number of the gangster's car at their disposal the next time they decided to pay him a visit at his bistro.

To Matt, it must've looked as if some type of poetic justice had just intervened in their favor for no sooner had Bill begun searching through the myriad numbers of computer files, he stated most enthusiastically that their prime suspect, one Gilford Minton, had just recently failed to appear in traffic court to answer for a speeding ticket he'd earned while driving ninety miles an hour on one of the local expressways. This then meant, of course, that not only had Mr. Minton's driving privileges been temporarily suspended, but that he now had an outstanding arrest warrant on the books for failure to appear.

Then just as quickly as they could, the two detectives signed out of the squad room and then hurriedly drove over to the chicken man's restaurant where they proceeded to park their unmarked police car about a block away from his café. They were, however, especially careful to park their car in a spot where they could keep a close eye on Minton's late model, shinny-red Cadillac convertible which was conveniently parked across the street from the gangster's restaurant.

Then after waiting patiently in their unmarked police car for only about an hour or so, Matt and Bill observed a young woman who after first exiting the restaurant then quickly climbed into Minton's car where she proceeded to make a U-turn in the middle of the street before parking the Cadillac directly in the front of the restaurant. Then just moments later, Minton himself came strolling out of the front door of the restaurant and then stood on the sidewalk for a another moment or so while he carefully surveyed the territory before getting into the driver's seat of his own car.

"We must be living right," Matt said, "and please correct me if I'm wrong, but if I'm not mistaken then Minton's driving privileges have been temporarily suspended."

"No sir, Matt, you're not mistaken, and luckily for us he's not only driving illegally, but he's also heading due west which is exactly the way our car is facing," Bill said.

Then precisely at that time the two detectives elected to simply tail the Cadillac for a few additional blocks in order to give the suspect a little extra time to get out of his own neighborhood before they placed the call into dispatch for assistance.

Thus just shortly there afterwards, the driver of the shiny-red Cadillac found himself almost completely surrounded by at least a half dozen marked patrol cars; and within another few minutes or so, the gangster, Gilford Minton, was then summarily placed under arrest for both failing to appear as a traffic offender and for driving on a suspended license.

Then once finally back at the district stationhouse, Minton was perfunctorily booked, mugged, and fingerprinted. However, his Cadillac was towed to the police impound garage so that the crime scene technicians could conduct some tests on the trunk and the interior of the car in hopes they could find some traces of blood stains, or any other types of physical evidence that might yield some positive results.

Without a doubt, the two detectives held a definite edge over their prime suspect; and just the act of having physical control over both his body and his automobile was extremely important to the detectives and especially since the suspect was unable to know just exactly what types of physical evidence that he might have unwittingly left in the interior of his car.

Seemingly, the wheels of justice were about to turn in the detective's favor for no sooner had Minton been officially booked and charged with the two traffic charges he was told that he was to be held for a seventy-two hour period on a charge of conspiracy to commit murder.

Amazingly, though, almost everybody in the stationhouse was absolutely flabbergasted when Minton voluntarily agreed to take a lie detector test. This new and strange development in the case was particularly vexing to Matt and Bill since Minton had already been advised that a suspect in a criminal matter cannot legally be forced to submit to a polygraph examination.

Nonetheless, once the technician had finished hooking Minton up to the polygraph machine, and then after they'd begun in earnest to ask the suspect some very pertinent questions about the recent homicide of a Southside gang member, the tech almost immediately came running back out of the interrogation room with the news that Minton had lied when answering almost every single question that he'd asked of him; and that, he'd even lied when asked for his true name.

Fortunately for Matt, however, he'd just recently read a memo that'd had come down from the Intelligence Division which had advised all of the technicians and the detectives to be sure to remove the suspect's shoes and socks before administering the polygraph test.

Then not so surprisingly, once the detectives had removed Minton's shoes and socks they found a long thumbtack that was protruding up through the bottom of his sneaker. Apparently, all Minton had to do was to push firmly down on his foot in order to make contact with the tack; and which in turn would cause him to feel an excruciating amount pain in the bottom of his foot. Without a doubt, the pain that the suspect would be forced to endure by pushing down on the tack would not only affect the machine's ability to distinguish the truth from a falsehood, but the disturbance caused by the pain in the suspect's foot would almost certainly cause the needle on the machine to run crazily up and down the page.

By then, Minton's little trick with the tack in the shoe was literally out in the open; and so naturally, he then very wisely refused to continue on with the polygraph examination.

Then at that point, Matt and Bill must have felt as if they owned Minton body and soul; or at the very least they had physical control over his body for the next three days. So then shortly thereafter the detectives placed the gangster in an interrogation room where they were planning to really go to work on him. Hence from then on, it was a simple matter for them to just flash some important looking lab evidence papers in the front of his face and then just let him sweat for a little while.

Regardless, though, , it wasn't long at all before Matt and Bill had exhausted all of their interrogative ploys on the man whom they both believed was responsible for at least one of the more recent gang related homicides on the Southside.

Therefore, they were more than a little thankful when their boss, Detective Lieutenant Martin Sorrels, knocked on the two-way mirrored glass window of the interrogation room where Matt and Bill were still in the process of questioning Minton.

Thus after stepping briskly out into the hallway to greet the Lieutenant, Matt was handed a report which stated that a pistol been found in a false compartment in the driver's-side door panel of Minton's Cadillac. Then after the gun in question had been test fired, it'd been determined that pistol found in the door of Minton's Cadillac was the actual murder weapon that was used to kill one of Minton's Westside rivals.

Then in addition to receiving the momentous news about the pistol that had just been recovered from Minton's car, the Lieutenant also informed Matt that the crime lab technicians had found some blood stains in the trunk of the Cadillac that matched the blood type of the young Southside gang member who'd recently been executed by his own associates.

So at that point in time Gilford Minton was officially arrested for the murder of one of his own gang members; and in addition to having to answer for that one specific charge of homicide, he'd also become the prime suspect in the murder of another young man who'd just recently been killed on the Westside of town.

Then not too surprisingly, once the Cook County Deputy District Attorney had explained to the gangster that in all likelihood he would become eligible for a needle in the arm, both Minton and his attorney very wisely decided to accept a plea bargain agreement for a sentence of life in prison without parole. There was, however, an additional part of the plea-bargain agreement for a lesser sentence which Minton would have to agree to if he wished to escape the death penalty; and that one very important stipulation was that he would have to give up the name of the gang member who'd killed the young boy named Yummy back in the year of nineteen hundred and ninety-four.

As Socrates once said, "All vice is based on ignorance, All virtue is based on knowledge."

The End

DETECTIVE
CHICAGO POLICE
CITY OF CHICAGO
INCORPORATED 4th MARCH 1837
213

EPILOGUE

At least according to the most knowledgeable of the modern-day prognosticators, the twenty-first century homicide detectives will not only have to be well experienced in the solving of homicides but they will also have to be well trained in the use of the latest cyberspace spy-technology. Though in his way of thinking, homicide detective Mathew Morris still fervently believes in the empirical methods of detection that he'd first learned from the numerous members of his own family who'd served with distinction on the Chicago Police Department as homicide detectives.

In the past, just the solving of a case of homicide was difficult enough; but nowadays, the modern-day detectives must also carry the additional burden of having to worry about the threat of international and domestic terrorists. And as the Federal Authorities have repeatedly warned us, no city in America, not even the ones located in the Midwest, could expect to be completely immune from the dangers of terrorism in this very unsettled 21st Century.

An example of just how unsettled this 21st Century is capable of being would be the incident of a former Russian spy who'd died a slow and agonizing death from radiation poisoning that he'd unwittingly ingested while having dinner in an upscale London, England restaurant. Consequently, then, that one case in point has further demonstrated the need for us to continue to focus our efforts on espionage, both foreign and domestic. And for our country's own sake it now seems more imperative than ever that we should intensify the training of our homicide detectives on how best to investigate such crimes as intentional radiation poisoning; then too, we must continue to stay on guard against the threat of a chemical warfare attack such as the use of the deadly chemical agent anthrax or even the fatal nerve gas called sarin.

Although luckily for the Chicago Police Department a good percentage of their more experienced homicide detectives have already received their training by the Department of Defense, the F. B. I., and the C. I. A. on specifically how best to investigate a home-grown act of terrorism. Accordingly then, a very select squad of investigators from that very same pool of detectives is now being headed by Detective Sergeant Morris of the Chicago Police Department's Homicide Division who has just recently been assigned to investigate the deaths of a few civilians who'd previously been employed at the U. S. Naval Military Reservation that's located on the Illinois border of Lake Michigan.

By chance, the pandemic, as it would have inevitably been labeled by the press, had so far been contained within the borders of the U. S. Navy's Great Lakes Training Center which lies just north of the city of Chicago. However, what with the number of civilians who currently work at the base, there always exists the very real possibility that the highly communicable disease which had already killed several people might eventually be contracted by a substantial number of the civilian population who live in or around the city of Chicago.

Therefore, when Detective Sergeant Mathew Morris of the Chicago Police Department's Homicide Division was asked to assemble a taskforce of detectives that would represent the different departments of law enforcement in the area which included both the Illinois

Counties of Lake and Cook, they also held meetings with the representatives from the various other governmental agencies which were primarily responsible for solving the murders of the innocent civilian workers at the U. S. Naval Installation.

Unfortunately, though, both the heads of the police departments and the civic administrators would soon find themselves at complete odds with the representatives of the U. S. Military. So from then on, whenever the local authorities attempted to interview one of the suspected terrorist who just happened to be a foreign national who'd migrated to the U. S. from another country, the civic authorities would almost invariably find that they had to endure the interference from the U. S. State Department.

More importantly, though, it was discovered that the terrorists who'd planned and then carried out the poisoning of the civilian workers at the U. S. Navy base were actually from a local homegrown cell of dissidents who'd been residing in the city of Chicago for a period of several years prior to the incident.

So naturally, the future looked troublesome for Detective Sergeant Mathew Morris and the rest of the local investigators who'd already been inducted into the multiple-government's anti-terrorism taskforce which had originally been created by the Chicago Police Department.

Accordingly, then, it was readily apparent to Detective Sergeant Mathew Morris that his life as he'd known it would never again be the same. For even with almost limitless assistance from the Federal Government, the city of Chicago was about to face a daunting task in its effort to uncover the secret lives of the well-entrenched homegrown terrorists who already had several years in which to blend in with society before some of their brethren had so brazenly attacked the United States on that fateful day in September of two-thousand and one.

So therefore, Mathew Morris, along with the other members of the Chicago Police Department's anti-terrorism task force, was about to face some unprecedented challenges that would require of them to discard their usual methods of investigating and interrogating suspected terrorists; and which then might also mean that the detectives on the newly formed task-force might just have to take a page out of the U. S. Government's book of rules by temporarily suspending the time-honored law of habeas corpus and the Geneva Conference's disdain for torture.

Then too, if the members of the city, county and state law enforcement agencies were to ever become successful in the capture of some of the yet unknown homegrown terrorists then the time might have come for them to also temporarily suspend certain parts of the U. S. Constitution and all of the other guidelines of warfare that were originally put into place to protect the innocent members of society.

Thus when faced with the greatest challenge of his life as an investigator, Detective Sergeant Mathew Morris knew full well that he would need every tool at his disposal if he ever planned on solving the case of the, "Poisonous Printer's Ink," which was the name that the F. B. I. and the media had appropriately given the material that'd been used to kill the civilian workers and the residents of Chicago in the latest terrorist attack on America.

AUTHOR'S BIO

Years ago, as I was putting the finishing touches on a project titled, "My family's History," the desire to put my creative thoughts on paper reemerged; and then once those creative thoughts had been unleashed from the deep recesses of my mind, there was no stopping me.

To be honest, however, the desire to write poetry and prose has always been a part of me; and even as far back as high school I can still vividly remember the day when I parked my car next to an advertising agency with the express idea of going inside and telling those people about my desperate need to write ads and jingles.

But instead of entering the building, I decided to wait until after I had finished college before attempting to find a job in the advertising industry. And also just as regrettably, I soon became so obsessed with my new position in the retail industry that I once again put my writing career on hold.

On the bright side, however, it was working in a junior department store in the city of Chicago, Illinois where I was to meet the Chicago Policemen who worked security in my store that would ultimately stimulate my imagination enough for me to write my crime fiction novel, "Chicago P. D. Homicide."

www.ingramcontent.com/pod-product-compliance
Lightning Source LLC
Chambersburg PA
CBHW070503120726
47910CB00003B/1110